I0531605

FINANCIAL THRILLER
THE DEAD BANK DIARY
SERIES

THE DEAD BANK DIARY

By Anna Schlegel

BOOK ONE

Translation from Russian

Schlegel Press Association

The Dead Bank Diary by Anna Schlegel
Book One of The Dead Bank Diary Series

Published by Schlegel Press Association
Friedrichstr. 123
Berlin, Germany 10117

ISBN: 9780986174902

First Edition: February 2015

Translated by Alla Koshechkina
Cover photography by Tom Grill /Corbis & Maxim Shirkov /Shutterstock

Also By Anna Schlegel
THE DEAD BANK DIARY SERIES

FOR THOSE IN THE SHADE

Book Two of The Dead Bank Diary Series

THE PRINTS ON THE SNOWS OF YESTERYEAR

Book Three of The Dead Bank Diary Series

SOME DAY I`LL HIT A BANK

Book Four of The Dead Bank Diary Series

THE FROZEN DEBT

Book Five of The Dead Bank Diary Series

MY GOD IS MONEY

Book Six of The Dead Bank Diary Series

Coming Soon

Also By Anna Schlegel
THE SLEEPER SERIES

MONEY CAN`T LIE

Book One of The Sleeper Series

ON MYSELF FOR LITTLE MONEY

Book Two of The Sleeper Series

Coming Soon

CONTENTS

AUTHOR'S NOTE

In these books there are no cops, no killings. There is much about the illegal takeover of banks, and a powerful lot of money. I know how to pump up a bank, and how to bankrupt a bank. I love beautiful gray schemes on the verge of crime. My stories are about fraud in the eyes of a swindler. There are no good guys.

I write about the golden-time bankers, from 1998, when neither the police nor the intelligence services, or any crimes haven't prevent the banks to make money.

These novels are not based on a true story, but you will face this reality in every word.

Anna Schlegel

The rats living on the refuse of the bank backyard stay
full at all times

THE DEAD BANK DIARY

This is not a robbery. A bank is taken with all its guts: accounts, debts, points of exchange, the staff to the last secretary, the building. This is beautiful and clean fraud.

I was out of work, while all around you could smell millions, even in the air outside. It was an unforgettable smell of public debt, oilfields, gold, bank guarantees, diamonds... I wanted to breathe in the air of easy cash Moscow, to revel and roll in this air. I could feel the smell of money in the wind on my face. This air was used to make up funds overnight, to make a fortune, to go rack and ruin and then grow rich again. It was going free across the wreckage of the sold out Soviet empire.

I was asked to help redeem the debts of a bank. The insider man at the bank held the post of Vice President.

A bit of danger and a bit of love.

ABOUT THE SERIES

These are stories about a man who is not alive anymore. He was a financier, a retired intelligence officer. I had the good luck to arrange a couple of financial frauds. We bumped into each other before the recession, in the flood of shit, together in the dust.

After his death I still had power of attorney.

Of course, Victor knew I wouldn't be able to work on his contacts. I had tried. Now it's funny to think of it. I am, and always have been, a go-between, a rat. Nobody needs middlemen. They get rid of them; they send them to Hell. But I had a white shirt with a necktie, and copies of million-strong contracts for oil, gas, diamonds, and rare-earth metals: light-as-air, rolled fax sheets with lots of zeroes. They made me giddy; they made me drunk. And I ran along with them, and easily foisted them for the middlemen: muddy, middle-aged misters.

When some of the first deals failed, I went into hysterics. I wanted to throw everything in.

Once I had a dream. In my dream, I heard a telephone call,

"Miss Schlegel? We need your signature to extend a contract concluded by Mr... "

I woke up scared; something turned over inside of me. I realized that I was spending my life waiting for such a call. It didn't matter where it caught me.

But there was no going back. Once you've taken a step forward, you realize you can't turn back anymore.

Why did he leave all this to me? I looked the papers over, recalling past years, deals, people, talks: everything from the first meeting to the last minute. And I couldn't find anything for me; because it wasn't for me, actually, for the old me. So I changed. I became a con.

My life was changed. Sometimes it was as convincing and disgusting as a life of a whore. It was as inaccessible as the man who despises you. It was like vomit or sweat from the body from heavy hangover shivers. You wish to run, and there's no place to run to. It's a cold stupor. So it's stupid to look at the smeared corpse on the road, and it's impossible to regain consciousness to look away. This passion nests in the heart, and you don't know what is it.

I have his photo, the last one, taken at Arkhangelskoe hospital. Summer. We're sitting on the edge of a dried-up fountain. He embraces me with one arm, and I'm lost next to him. He is gray-haired and corpulent. He has a mocking look. And behind us there are towering white marble angels.

CHAPTER ONE

IGOR

Moscow, June 1998

Igor, an ex-intelligence serviceman was waiting for me at Chinatown Metro station. He had a swollen red face with insane bloodshot, drunken eyes. He smelled of sweat and alcohol; his face was burning. When he was drunk he looked like a bevvied bedbug, as if he'd sprinkle blood in your face if you pressed on him. He grasped me by the elbow with his sticky hot palm and turned me to face him. He was speaking in his usual manner, eye to eye. I kept listening, without looking away from the bloody gaze of his eyes, where blindly, like a fly in netting, beat the apple of his eye. I got used to this. He was bluffing. Even sober Igor lied wholeheartedly, with confidence and without shame, like children do.

Catching up on some crazy story on a night flight with five million dollars in exchange for rubles, and a platoon of machine gunners, he added casually just to make sure,

"I got a wooden leg. Want to see it unfastened?"

"Here, stop flirting."

I slightly pushed him away, sneaking out my elbow.

"Why, you don't believe me? You know where I had to fight?"

We came out of the train into the grasping blind heat. The sun was falling blindly all over the place; there was no shelter, no chance to rest my eyes in some shade. Everything was equally lit with dim, white sunlight. Igor's white shirt made me blink; I had no wish to lift my eyes. My glance stopped at his moist red neck bearing beads of sweat. I had no wish to listen to Igor. He was talking of his being wounded in Chechnya and how he lost his leg. Pure bullshit. His leg was well intact and hairy.

Everyone knew he got his worst injury from his wife. Having learnt of his adultery, she hit his balls with the sharp toe of her shoe. Fright, pain, swelling: all was gone a long time ago. But for a good while after, when putting his hand in his pocket, he was still imperceptibly scratching his healing ball. This habit remained: some male instinct made him thrust his hand into a pocket and touch it, to make sure it was all safe and sound inside, and then slightly scratch it.

However, he loved his wife. He had been with her for twenty years. He was always living alone in different places, but did his best to visit her with a sober mind, and not empty-handed. Like many others, having seen so much death, he was artless and naïve. He felt uneasy coming to see her with nothing. Unnoticed, he would pull a five-hundred note from his wife's purse, and seating himself at the table, hand it over to her, saying, *Well, that is all I have until they open me a credit line.*

She started hiding her purse and marking the notes, so Igor imperceptibly turned into an alcoholic.

It was absolutely impossible to make any deals with Igor. How did he draw me into this currency exchange?

Eventually, we made it. The bank was on some industrial site. Their hall was empty. At the doors it reeked of the heat from the street, with its sugary smell of cob brick. Imbecile as he was, Igor and I were not allowed in for negotiations.

After some fooling around Igor went up to a young female clerk,

"Listen, I'm a veteran. I lost my leg. I've got to pee."

And he was allowed upstairs. From what Igor heard hanging around the conference room, the deal was bollocks. The bank could not accept money into their depository. There used to come an armored vehicle full of cash, the money was counted and then the vehicle left for the depository of Guta-Bank for exchange. The vehicle would come back, and the cash recounted. But at the time of exchange at Guta-Bank the cash was left unattended by security. Two hours of talks and bargaining...

Leaving the bank we both concurrently spat.

"Let's pee over here!" Igor waved sideways, towards the dusty shrubs.

My cell started ringing. It was Nikita. His voice was hardly getting through the noise of the airport, far away.

"Ann, listen. You know here in the airport I met some guy and he died. Just a normal guy, we just talked a little. It seems he was a courier. It just so happened I've got his parcel. There was an old bond of a million dollars inside. I sent it to

Arcady's address by DHL. It will soon come. Go get it put through... "

"Nikita, how did it happen you've got that bond on you?"

"I took it accidentally."

"You mean you stole it? You know what you put foot in...?" I screamed, as if I wanted to thunder down into the airport hubbub that was creeping into my head.

"Not stolen. I took the parcel and thought to give it over to... There was no address. So you get it through... " Nikita cut me short, "I am no good at bonds. So see you, they have announced my flight number."

He rang off.

"Igor... this bloody idiot has stolen a million-dollar bond ...and sent it to Arcady. A million dollars in one note! How do you like this shit?"

"Your ass is going to be the shooting mark," Igor clicked his tongue.

"Let's get to Arcady's place fast."

"I don't care where we drink vodka," said Igor, "And Nikita is a walking shithouse, so all kinds of shit sticks well on him."

We exchanged looks unwittingly and quickened the pace.

At Arcady's house, in the black archway, a dog rushed by, dirty yellow like the evening sun on the asphalt. I used to see him here quite often. The dog darted out in a shivery bent silhouette, soaked the corner with a fine jet, sparkling for a second in the sun, and then he ran away, hopping and looking back. I threw my head up. From below one could notice the windows wide open, the dim crystal chandelier over the table, flashed scraps of some visitors, juniper smoke coming out.

Arcady used to burn birch logs and juniper in his fireplace, and grill kebabs. There was no big gathering, however the rooms were filled with scuffling, the sound of chairs getting set back, the clinking of dinnerware, and the rusting of husky smokers' voices coming from the stairwell. People walked out to smoke, the street door incessantly creaking and banging on its old over-strained door spring, letting the smoke puffs inside, heavy echoes coughing in the depths of the corridor.

The stairway always smelled of mildew, having the reek of stale humid air. I used to recognize Arcady by this rugged odor ground-in everything in his apartment, and engrained in him, his clothes and hair. I could feel it in the street and in the metro. The sun has dried the walls and the mildew smell has somewhat faded away.

Somehow most people managed to adjust to this kind of life, but Arcady could not. Having lost their ministerial portfolio, some of them went into business in undergarments. Arcady however, after losing his deputy chair in a huge corporation, still could not find his place. Arcady was trading in useful contacts. He was either getting old or lazy. One way or another, he was damned to make people meet and get his fees on such brokerages.

Arcady was not my father, but we had been close since childhood; I got his habits, and he was the dearest person in my life.

Today, Arcady was winding up some of his bric-a-brac, quite a lot, in order to repurchase another apartment. That is, the apartment of his brother residing abroad. Arcady was accustomed to consider it his own property, all the more because these apartments were just next door.

"Arcady!"

My voice got lost in the depths of his corridor.

Arcady was tall and lean. He had a tired face with boyish features, with olive eyes, and with old-fashioned goatee, lively and fluid, easily changing from squeamish satiety to children's gluttony.

"This is for you," Arcady handed me a bulky envelope.

From the envelope pattered out a doubled old bond exposing its worn out folds to the light. Right in the center was an oval portrait of Ulysses S. Grant, just like on a fifty-dollar bill. The upper frame of the portrait was decorated with frostwork monograms, slightly obliterated in the middle. Under the portrait there were coupons laid in rows. The old paper was amazing: it was issued by the Federal Reserve System of the United States in 1934, for one million dollars. So many zeros! The note warmly lit up in the light, showing its watermarks, and somewhat changed its color from paludal to grass-green.

Involuntarily I rubbed my cheek against it. It felt a little crusty, like a shelf-warmer atlas, a little hardened with humid air. I could even smell out a subtle stale odor like that usually coming from long-time packed old clothes in the flea market, or last year's leaves dumped under the snow. And then there was a smell as if hundreds of human fingers had touched it before. It was so abraded and crumpled that it seemed it had changed hands over and over again.

And I do love the odor of cash! I just liked how money smells. I used to enjoy tumbling even a one-hundred note in my palms, and then unwittingly bringing it right to my nose. Oh! This note, however, smelled of something unusual. This must be the smell of big money.

Bullshit! I had never seen one million dollars in a single note. In was such a big and beautiful note... and with so many coupons.

The envelope also contained some other faxed cover letters. They said: the US Federal Reserve Bonds were issued prior to the Bretton Woods Agreement of 1944 by the US Government as US gold bonds to be traded in exchange for money to third parties or used to repay a debt. The United States Government guaranteed these bonds with US gold reserves.

The cover letters also included the Gold Bullion Certificate and the Treasury Certificate, where the US Treasury confirmed the relevant gold security amount and quality. The whole lot was enclosed with a Global Immunity Certificate.

The Global Immunity copy read: In virtue of the power in them here unto enabling the United States of

America to determine and to contract in a manner appearing as a loan which shall be known as US Federal Reserve Bonds series 1934. The locator and redeemer will be free from criminal offense and be duly covered by complete immunity documented for the safety of all parties concerned.

The bearer of these bonds acts as a lender while the United States Government acts as a debtor. For over fifty years these bonds have been in free circulation. They were free from charges, mortgage or other encumbrance by third party rights. No rejection of claim on the part of the United States was acceptable, nor withdrawal of debt acknowledgement.

All this text came undersigned and sealed.

Bullshit. If the bond itself were a faxed copy I would rather think it was no better than another 10-million dollar Fed, a copy of which I'd just recently had on my hands. It was still somewhere lost among other copies.

I remembered having crumpled up this paper with the intention of casting it into the wastepaper basket, but I still changed my mind, thinking I could come across it again after a long while, and smile. With a similar feeling, I had folded and kept my old luxury dress in the wardrobe. There was nowhere to dress up.

It was out of fashion. But still I could accidentally see it while sorting out my wardrobe, and remember those nonchalant and wealthy times, so I could cry hiding my face in that robe.

"Handsome forgery. I didn't know it could be so good. Just as good as real," said Igor, taking the bond to his eyes, and fumbling it against the light. "At one time there were many of this kind in the market. So many we were sick and tired of."

"You think it's the same fake note?" I was disappointed.

"Really handsome! Wonderful! A million dollars in one note! A bearer bond! Never seen anything better." Igor laughed. "And you what were you thinking?"

"I was thinking the same until I took a smell... that smell... it smells of money! It smells of a million dollars!"

"It smells of crime," chuntered Igor, handing the bond to Arcady.

"And this is not the fake note that used to be out in the market," Arcady said, "This one is different. That note had a 100-million dollar face value. Don't you remember? But Fed has never issued anything worth over one million. And this one is exactly one million. Humble indeed. Never thought I'd be holding it in my hands. I heard these bonds were used to repay Russian national debt."

"How many of those were there?" I asked.

"Up to twenty billion worth," Arcady said, recollecting that story. "I am not an expert of course, but... Michael, you are not yet going?" cried out Arcady in the kitchen way.

"Michael?"

I was thinking Arcady made up his mind to sell another print by Falck, cherished against a rainy day, and this was why he was calling for Michael. I looked at him uneasily, but Arcady just waved me aside and smiled. Michael was only coming to chat and kick the tires.

Michael, a fine art expert and connoisseur, was sitting in the corner of the kitchen with his bony arms crossed and his fingers intertwined with a smoldering cigarette. From afar he seemed tied up in a knot. He stood up, going round mindlessly, moving sweepingly like a stuffed doll. He approached, his face with high cheekbones sinking under grey temples, clicked the lighter and knotted up again, sat next to me.

By the way, with all his shapelessness it turned out Michael was attractive to females. In his youth, Michael would strike in the face without much talking. He would only take off his specs. And he never cashed in on his clients. He was an original, as per one of his friends' evaluations.

Arcady pushed away some teacups with a motion of his hand from the table corner.

"Here, look, Michael, what a wonderful forgery!"

Arcady unfolded the bond in front of him.

Michael took the bond paper close to his eyes, narrowing and flickering up and down the monograms as if probing them.

"Unbelievable. It's a work of art," he whispered over the note.

"All American bonds of that time look similar to this one. And dollars too." It didn't ring any bells with Arcady.

"I haven't seen any others, Arcady. And this one was not done yesterday. It's from between 1940 and 1960. This banknote is a real masterpiece. And if it's a forgery, it is obviously by a famous forger."

"Who must be dead by now," Igor remarked.

"That is for the better. So his name is a long time well known to everyone. His style and touch looks familiar to me, over here... " Michael carefully tapped on with his bony finger the conglomerate of white monograms intertwined as a knot of worms, drifted to the upper edge of the line curved just above the portrait.

"Style and touch? On a bond paper?" Arcady asked again dubiously.

"Just like the master's style and touch... You know the touch of a certain painter never gets changed, just like his fingerprint. No matter what he paints, or money... The touch remains. I visited an exhibition of the Russian painter Smirnov in The Tretyakov Gallery three years ago. It was brought from Austria. There is a museum of his with all his works there. And you know what? Smirnov used to make handmade dollars. He would wash off the ink from a one-dollar note and make a hundred instead. He served his time in jail, came out. Lived under a different name, kept refreshing his documents and died in Vienna... And his touch was remarkable."

Michael went to search for his spectacles, took his magnifier. And for a rather long time, adjusting the specs and the magnifier, he kept looking with his keen eyes at the bond.

"What is there to look at, Michael?" Igor wondered, uncomprehending.

"If I hadn't known the hand of Smirnov so well, I would take it for a genuine bond. That would be a real bond for anyone else."

"Really? Why are you so sure of that?"

"There is a misprint, have a look here," Michael slightly touched on the text. "Such misprints used to be intentionally made by, say, the Bank of England. I am sure the Fed allowed for this misprint to distinguish a real bond from a fake one. That means the fraudster must have been holding a real bond in his hands."

"Let us have a drink," Igor poured him some whiskey.

"Yeah, we'd rather have a drink," agreed Michael, taking off his specs and putting aside the bond paper. "But, I had better smoke... "

Michael kept smoking grass out of his college-time habit when appraising an unknown artwork by sight.

"It's immaterial what kind of note this is," voiced Arcady in a frigid and sober tone, "What is important, is that every bond has its owner. No matter if its payable to bearer or not. And the owner is now looking for it."

And he was right: all promissory notes, all papers, forgery or not, meant a real person with actual or paper funds. And if the paper funds, like this bond case, were too big; that meant the money owner was a millionaire.

This had nothing to do with the long-time deceased forger. The bond belonged to a live person. This bond came out not by chance. It must have dropped out of a deal, of a major transaction, where it would get exchanged for something, and go back to sleep in the bank depository vault for many years. This was not a market transaction. It appeared to be a deal between two parties who knew each other well. The bond could be getting transferred from one bank to another. So the transaction was aborted. It might have been a million dollar deal.

"Well, that's real shit. So who may be the owner?" Igor asked, following Arcady.

"It's hardly a criminal transaction," Arcady started speculating. "The criminal world was not allowed to buy up the government debt. This should be the intelligence agency case. We'd better find the owner fast. And give the bond back. It's just like keeping a bomb under the bed."

"And how do you find the owner?" I wondered.

"Well if you don't find him, he will find you, and that'll be worse," retorted Arcady.

"Let us find the body in the first place," resolved Igor. "The courier died at the airport? Let's go there."

CHAPTER TWO

MESCHANKA STREET

It was easy to find out where the body of a young man who died in the airport was transferred to. It turned out he died of a heart attack. There was nothing strange about it.

In the hospital I told the doctor on duty the story of my friend getting acquainted with the young man in the airport, and their exchange of wristwatches for good luck. My friend went on a business trip abroad having left this watch to me.

"If someone wants it as a memento I will give it away," I said, holding out my business card.

The business card read that I was an Investment Group trader. Overleaf I dropped a line to come in person, so that the person who wanted the bond knew that I was fully aware of what fell into my hands, of its value, and my ability to dispose of it.

There was some time to go.

Igor and I, we placed the bond in the bank safety deposit box registered in his name. I did not ask why he decided to do so. I did not want to hear the reply.

"I'll stay with you," resolved Igor, "I don't think that this will take long... "

I was renting an apartment in Meschanka Street, in a modest three–storey building located in the depths of a courtyard opening at the Garden Ring Road, cleaving unto the rear facades of the high residential blocks overlooking the road. From the road my house looked like a fragment among the even rows of robust yellow teeth of the Stalin development era. And still one could hardly sleep without the incessant drone of the main road.

The apartment fell to my lot rather cheaply. As per the documents, the building should have been demolished ten years ago. There should have been another house built, but the investor rejected the project and the building was under continuous legal proceedings. The house remained abandoned, dust-laden, with bare windows bearing no curtains, their darkness being an eyesore from afar. Those who rented apartments here had no money for curtains. The house was like a phantom in the downtown.

Just recently the house had the gas cut off. And right after that, the house's wealthy inhabitants started moving out. As we approached, there was yet another family moving out. At the entrance, under the roomy Toyota trunk plenty of boxes were heaped up, and a beautiful mastiff languished in the heat. The narrow staircase smelled of sweet onion patties, and was all cluttered with various belongings. One more family was getting ready to move out.

"You haven't sold the tea yet?" asked Igor, entering my apartment.

A fifty-kg bag of tea was kept in the corner. It had to be sold. This tea was excess from my friend's store in Petersburg. Initially the tea bag seemed to occupy half the room space, so big it was. However within a week, my neighbors had pulled it apart and the bag mildly shrunk, its tightly-packed tummy getting somewhat limp. But the heavy odor of stale hay was still thick and low to the ground, interposing all other smells in the apartment and leaking into the communal stairway. My neighbors from the ground floor also came to ask for tea. Outdoors, both my shirt and hair held the scent of this tea.

The tea was my night-hag. I had nowhere to get away from it, had I? I called the Department of Corrections. In jail, tea had to be as good as gold. But it turned out the Department of Corrections had too many calls daily.

Igor passed directly to the kitchen, and with a rattle of a master hand, he started taking out glasses and plates, making sandwiches. After a drink of vodka, and hardly a snack, he was soon snoring on my sofa like a tractor in the fields.

I heard my fax beep, and rushed to get the message. And it was the same every day. The fax blurted out heaps of white paper, so many it seemed to be snowing. It kept pouring and pouring multi-million poisons that I kept devouring all day long till late, to a drunken stupor. And in the morning again I came seeking it, suffering with the thirst of a hangover. I picked up the rolled white sheets crispy in my fingers, and gazed into the lines of multiple zeros crooked and creepy like bird traces on the snow.

Every bloody day started the same. My calls were all the same. Same kind of talk.

"Vladimirovich, hello! Break stone? From which pit is that? Yeah, let me think. You haven't got a hundred bucks till tomorrow?"

"Ivanovich? I'm fine, thanks. Yes, let's talk about the oil promptly. See you in Chinatown, as usual. And who did you say is there? A middleman? Hmm... Let's do it this way. He'll be getting his fee on every shipment, but no earlier. Hundred tons shipped, let him get his hundred ton fee. Could I borrow a hundred bucks?"

"That's me, Konstantinovich. Oh, fine! So what have you got? Twenty million bank guarantee? Okay, let's meet. In the Chinatown cafe. And could you lend me a hundred bucks till Monday?"

"Petrovich! I'm good. So what have you got? Foreign Currency Bonds of 2001? What's the amount? Five billion dollars? And the split? Hundred thousand each... Your buyer is ready to produce cash? The bid is approved by the Foreign Trade Bank for the first tranche?... Good. Any chance you got a hundred dollars?"

"Tea. Low-grade. In bags, per fifty kg. Carriage to Moscow... "

I chose this lifestyle myself. My choice was to moon over millions.

So much has changed over the recent years of freedom and national collapse, since those holy times when money came on a dripping roast. And only the bone-lazy wouldn't open their mouth to get his catch. And today, misery has driven off the million-mooners just like me into the offices of all kinds of companies. They were getting their end-of-month wages now, and seemed to have forgotten the taste of easy cash. They have forgotten how money makes you drunk. The dizziness from it... The traders who used to work with me on the stock market in that investment company, and all those bank clerks, none of them had learnt anything about this. It was just like living and never getting to learn a thing about life.

Once I was fired, I never searched for another job. That would have been ridiculous. Everything around me smelled of millions; it was in the air. It was the unforgettable smell of government debt, oilfields, gold, bank guarantees, diamonds... They wouldn't breathe it in. They wouldn't poison their life with it. They would speak to me as if they were bringing me to the door and giving me a kick in the ass. They were right in their own way. They were making their daily bread. All of them were married with children, dogs, cars to service... they had so many other things. Their brains were jammed full with small money, chock-full of petty cash. If we tried to stick a million dollars in their heads, they would explode. Or fall apart like an old birdhouse.

So, for my old friends remaining in the stock market, I was more of a leper. Or rather, stone dead, smelling of sweetly rotting flesh.

This must have been the smell that prevailed among those dealt in nothing but thin air. To say the old would not do nickel and dime, or to tear them apart just because they could see better, or were far more experienced? No. Not at all. Rather, they looked powerless to me. They were not after millions for the sake of those millions alone. They were not after bare cash bite. They wanted to do business. They were not used to being just kicked out of the business circle. And still, they were the old. It seemed to me, among those who traded a thin air I was among the dead. And it felt really bad, for me as a live being. But I shared their way of thinking. I was just like them. Ridiculous and old-fashioned, useless clutter, rubbish. Market garbage. And when I felt myself dead, it got better. Life got better.

I have inconspicuously breathed in the poison in full. I got that million-mooner disease. I kept hiding it for a rather long time though, like people hide their alcohol abuse or drug addiction. And then it made no difference. Everything changed: my talking, gestures, habits. I liked being another person, being a soulless, fussy creep running after big money.

I raised up nothing but multiple contacts, whom I kept asking for money on trust. I was lucky, having remained out of work. I soon realized I would never get a job.

Everything I thought important in life suddenly went down in value and lost its point. I could have some food or stay hungry, as long as I had my cigarettes and vodka.

My face was plain, pale, and bitter; my eyes looked hungry, and my shoes were whacked out. My contacts were just like me: muddy middle-aged misters, continuously asking for money and bumming cigarettes.

I sometimes caught a strange look on myself, but then forgot about it. Megalopolis stirred me with a crowd and cleaned from their memory. There was no need to be nice, as kind people who talk with clients and colleagues daily. I had different way of talking. My talking always led to a deal. And in case it didn't, I said, *Fuck you*, and forgot about the person as if shaking off dust. That's all.

Nothing to regret. I had nothing to blame myself for. Dogs wouldn't blame themselves for their dog's life, would they? Sometimes one of my friends would remark, *You are not bored with dealing in millions?*

No. This made no difference.

I just couldn't fritter away my life, which was self-contained like a million dollars in one note. I couldn't break it up into dollars for my snacks in MacDonald's or China-made garments, for a commonplace life... That would be plain worthless.

I wanted to feel free. To breath in the air of easy cash in Moscow, to revel and roll in this air. Feel it on my face just like snow, etching into the skin and as biting as glass, or soft and slick, licking and dripping as watery spit.

And well, how could others not understand this time would go fast? Would they not realize this air has come for a short while only? And its flavor was not from around here. Out of this air, funds were made up overnight, to make a fortune, to go rack and ruin and grow rich again. It was going free across the wreckage of the sold out Soviet empire. I had to be fast.

Dealing in thin air wouldn't bring anything. Those who managed to make a fortune were told to just be lucky. And formerly, it had been a lottery indeed. But now it was no more. And many people had understood. There were also people reluctant to understand. They would keep running around like rats. And thank god they were there!

That night Arcady called me and said his contacts wanted me to help them buy out the debt of some defense companies. I knew the plant director in person and could speak to him right away.

"And who is asking?" I asked.

"He's an ex-officer of the Foreign Intelligence Service. Retired long time ago. They say he's a good bloke. Got an office in Arbat area," returned Arcady.

"What do you think?" I asked, shaking Igor awake by his shoulders.

"I think the guy who lost that bond won't be speaking to you like that. He'll be coming right here."

That night, breathing in the stale and heavy air infused with the tea, I was thinking I'd have to sell that fucking tea.

CHAPTER THREE

VICTOR

In the morning Igor and I approached an old humble two-storey mansion on Nikitsky Boulevard, with a wrought iron gate and dust-laden windows. The drizzle touched my face.

"I'll be right here in a cafe," said Igor, waving his hand towards the other side of the boulevard, "Call me in an hour or just come out."

"You worried?"

"Yeah, goddamn. You left your phone number a day ago, and still no one called you. That means there'd be no calls. He'll come."

This mansion used to be overstuffed, I thought, opening the pass door. At some time overstuffed with its well-fed and sleek owners, the mansion was now on the decline. Everything was aged and used up.

However, it still preserved the fragrance of the party meetings, of sulky Volga cars drifting off its entrance with their sunken croup, of Yugo- made shoes, and of puff pastry from its snack bar. The lobby, with its old parquet floor, crunched like sand between the teeth as the ladies walked upon it.

"I'm here for Victor Vladimirovich. I've got an appointment," I dropped to the guard, presenting my passport.

From the guard post window I could only see the shoulders marked with captain straps, and his hands like a blind man scouring across my passport lines. Then his hand leaned out of the window and waved at the entrance door.

"Ah... here he comes."

I left for the courtyard. It started raining heavily. The rain came against the pavement splashing into a slimy jelly rattle. Victor's black Opel was entering the gate, leisurely making a U-turn in front of the mansion. I came up to the car and found my own reflection in its tinted glass. A hungry look, and sticky wet hair.

With a click, the car door opened.

"Hello Victor. Nice to meet you; I'm Anna."

Victor nodded, and for a split second I saw in front of me, eye to eye, his dark face with heavy features, worn out and bloated, as if staling over the winter season, coarse and inveterate. He was in his sixties, with arched and wrinkled lips, and his light cold eyes vanished in the dark circles and behind his black eyebrows. He had a quizzical, loutish glance.

He came out of the car. I held up my head. He was huge. His face got instantly wet with the rain. He banked it up and dropped.

Tcha... that is a mature bull, I thought, looking at him breaking into a grin, showing his yellow tooth holding a crumpled filter tip. *Would be nice to bed him.*

He was unlike my usual counterparts. I felt his hands had touched big money. I could feel the money smell in his cheap cigarette.

Victor was looking at me in disappointment.

"And those defense contracts for Arcady... I was told they were coming through you?" he asked, choosing his words.

There you are. Defense contracts for Arcady. Someone told him I have slept with all three managers of the defense companies. Victor must have been expecting a sexy blonde with nice boobs.

"Yeah, but that was a long time ago. You are working with the defense companies, Victor?"

He passed his eyes over my face, as if trying to understand whether he missed something, and, holding my shoulder, turned me to the entrance door.

"Let's go talk, honey bunny."

His jacket was permeated with cheap smoke. He smelled of booze enough to bite. He must have had a bottle of vodka for breakfast.

We got to the second floor of his office, its windows blind with the rain. There was an ashtray on the windowsill filled with butts smoked off to the end.

"So what are you working on, honey bunny?"

I said to myself, *Excellent. He asked that. But I had to get in the know right away.*

If it were some of my other counterparts I would respond, "I'm dealing with the people who are interested in precious stones and rare metals. I got an agreement with the State Repository for Precious Metals for two billion dollars. That's a good deposit for any European financial instrument. Maybe we could subsequently take a place on the opening Diamond Exchange..."

Or I could say, "I've got a few diamond lots in progress, seven lots of rough diamonds, alexandrite, sapphires, and two emerald lots. And some rough stones, emeralds, over half a ton. The meeting in the bank went behind the scenes. There was me and the loan department manager..." And I would finish with, "By the way, would you lend me a hundred bucks?"

"So what are you working on, Victor?" I said in return.

Victor delved into his inside pocket and took out some crumpled copies of Pre-Advice, letter of intent or, as they say, preliminary authorization. Standby and other papers.

"Look here. How do you like it? This is deposit for a million. I'm getting this papers from Switzerland."

I unfolded the glossy fax paper with the blurred lines and peered into the text and signatures: We, Credit Suisse, hereby irrevocably acknowledge and confirm with our full bank responsibility the validity of the assets... We confirm that these assets have been verified and authenticated by us with full responsibility... On behalf of the Board of Credit Suisse, signature and seal, Zurich, Switzerland.

It was unbelievable. These were indisputable papers, issued in the name of Victor.

I caught myself daydreaming. The figures were too high. Were those papers non-counterfeit! Wow, one million... Why would he show it to me? Just teasing or probing? And what's his interest in? What is this talk? Is this just idle talk? Some people were talking of millions and billions just like politics. I liked talking about it myself. I didn't know what to think.

The reality I felt about Victor suddenly melted in the familiar multi-million air. I have had enough of this to last me a lifetime, ad nauseam.

"I wouldn't work on these papers," I said cautiously, still looking dumb at the bank details and the lines of zeros, unable to leave hold of them.

I wanted to show him I was fed up with these millions and was now dealing in real things. And the subject was dropped for me, just like for any bank trader.

"What, this is the first time you are holding a Pre-Advice in your hands?" he uttered indifferently, pulling out the papers from my fingers, and folding them back into his pocket.

"No, this is the second time."

The answer flew unwittingly as I remembered a Pre-Advice in Arcady's hands. He grinned loutishly. It disturbed me.

"When I had a Pre-Advice, every second room of the Intourist Hotel was occupied by a person who came to see me for business!" I blew up with a mighty heave.

He cackled shortly, dropped his jaw showing his yellow teeth. My god, it was such a shame.

Victor took a bottle of cognac from his office desk and poured a little into my glass.

"Drink. Welcome, company."

"Keep well, Victor," I had the drink and shriveled.

"So what are you working on? And what's wrong with my Pre-Advice?" he asked, pouring me more cognac.

A lighted clicked in his fingers. We got to smoking.

"Well, nobody here works with those deposits. You may put in pledge the Kremlin; no one would give a cent... "

"Why so? Say I come to a bank. I wanna pledge my underpants. Here you are. It's a million's worth. No problem. Done. I got to issue..."

"Victor, there has never been a case of underpants having raised more than their actual cost, which is ten rubles. There are things like listings and independent appraisal. As per the independent appraisal, Victor, your underpants would not make more than ten rubles... And the bank could issue a safekeeping receipt such as a mere notice of receipt just like they do in the railway station luggage room. You hand in your luggage and get this fact acknowledged. Only, there is more security involved. The bank got to have the money. And real big money! Keep well..." I had a drink.

"Well you know when I'm told the correspondent of a Siberian village bank could confirm something, I would not believe that. And when the correspondent is respectable that's a totally another story. That is, when a Swiss bank issues a safekeeping receipt, such paper is no more than a mere butt wipe, but a fully responsible financial instrument. So this bank is eligible to confirm my underpants cost a million; and yours, by all means, only ten rubles. And then it makes no difference weather my bank's got money or not. And whether I snagged my underpants or not."

"Fuck it, Victor. Fucked up. I was looking at your papers... "

"Why so fucked up?" he asked angrily, pouring out the cognac.

"By Western standards there is no fucking capital in none of our banks. Well, maybe some REEs or diamonds... "

Smiling, I looked at Victor. He kept silent, and I felt uncomfortable with that silence. Catching his cold and heavy eye for a split second resting on me as if pressing me down, it shot across my mind he wasn't checking things out for himself. Dammit... He liked me. That's it. I felt sultry. Beads of sweat instantly came on my nose and my upper lip.

I moistened my lips and swallowed hard, stuck in my throat with the cigarette smoke. Dammit. I was thinking, hoping, he won't be asking anything now, or I may respond in a strange voice.

"Just drink it and smoke," he lit up a cigarette for me and fitted it into my unwillingly opened lips.

I thought at the back of my mind, *Well, I hope I just got a job.*

Then some kind of trotting noise came down the corridor, followed by a knock of knuckles on the doorpost.

CHAPTER FOUR

TAKEOVER THE BANK

The door was pushed open and a frayed, grizzled gentleman came in. His jacket was open and smelling of rain. He kept his old briefcase under his arm.

"Ahhh... Peter! Goody! Please meet Anna. It's through her that Arcady got the defense contracts," Victor nodded to the frayed gentleman. "Here, please meet the Deputy Chairman Mr. Bykov Peter Petrovich," he presented the man, "Peter, give her your business card."

"Goody Victor!" lively smile from the banker, opening his soft gnarled toothless mouth and handing me his business card.

"Nice to meet you... Ehh... Hmm... Hasn't that bank died yet?" I almost bit my tongue.

"You won't believe it; it's still there!" the banker responded gaily. He was speaking fast and excitedly, "They were about to wimp it out. So, through the Central bank I brought up the question of support to this bank, to prevent its license revocation. And then I come to the bank, ask for the balance sheet and get the balance of Jan 1st. So I look at it, and it makes my hair curl! I tell the man I want a million dollar transfer by cash letter, so give me the tariff. And he asks me, which tariff? You ever met such an idiot? So I ask for the customer account, what company, and how much funds there. You can imagine? He refused. That's the new young board! Those bastards! And for a whole week no one would bring me coffee or cigarettes, not a single pack. They say, bring some money and then we'll see. I record all that for my own reference... "

"Fuck the bank. The bank won't give a single fuck. Peter is currently establishing in that bank," Victor started making things clear, "There is total replacement of the bank team underway."

I gave the banker a closer look. He was highly active, but somewhat tumbled or frayed. No, actually worn out. Over sixty age. His grey grown locks stared over his ears, wrinkled forehead and deeply receding hairline. His nose planted into mournfully curved eyebrows, and was held it high over the nose bridge repeating it manifolds making it also wrinkled. In a soft wave it arched and curved as if rare raindrops coming after rain. Some teeth were missing, with the remaining uncared-for rotten stumps revealed provincialism.

He was talking with a spray of spit coming out of his mouth like a leaky bucket,

"The board will get totally changed. All but Ilya, he'll stay. I'll have the primary signature authority. The new team is coming to the bank. This is the third team already. There have been two others before, who haven't done a thing. Fuck! Such a mess! At one time, the bank rolled out the offsets with the defense plants. Where did the money go? It's still not clear. You can't simply plunder that much. The bank operators are sitting around doing nothing. There is a front office, which is high time to send on its way, where the girls are leggy, I'm telling you that, Victor! Ilya collecting his *corps de ballet* there, or something, that old ass? They've got twenty exchange points around Moscow, and the bank's got no funds. Think of it?"

An involuntary thought flashed, *So how did you get to see the legs there, you old foozle?*

I cautiously raised my eyes to him with curiosity, and the banker smiled back to me with a serene wet and toothless smile.

"You got something to smoke?" Victor asked him.

"Yeah, there," the banker produced two packs of cheap cigarettes from his briefcase and placed them on the table.

Victor got the door open and called his secretary. She brought more cognac and snacks, and poured out tea. We drank some cognac.

"Should take over that bank. By any means," Peter said as fast as before, and thanked the secretary with an old-fashioned nod.

"So how do we take it?"

Victor dropped his question in perfect silence. Not a single rustle. The echo of his words sounded in my empty and suddenly sober mind.

I thought, *Oh bullshit! Smother the bank... But they seemed to be making no decision. Things are sorted by big money. Had to probe them for funds...*

"We need a 'pocket bank' to rest the money in. We anyway need it. Just imagine it, girl," the banker said with a black, hollow smile, "our millions landing in your bank account in a bank. Any bank. The bank will go bust! The bank owner will simply pocket the cash and run. And then go to Interpol to search for him all across Europe."

These words felt heart-easing, as if having one's death reprieved. I started smoking.

The old man was right. A 'pocket bank' was required. Getting major amounts transfer through other banks involved high risks. A banker used to counting peanuts at the sight of big money would have the temptation to grab it, run away and get lost. When a bank is not tailor-made for a major customer, it will only get thousands of minor depositors and rip them off. Local banks were all mere exchange shops. Here, the matter was of a one-time transaction, so the bank had to be under control.

"So why this bank, Peter?" I inquired, cursing myself for stupidity.

He didn't pay attention to this.

"This one just got drawn, so... firstly, it's cheap. Secondly, its staff have been caught stealing before, and are expected to face a criminal charge. The Auditing Chamber may come with an inspection any minute. While the bank's got a fairly good record: in the olden times they used to have a fluid capital, and also international status. So this bank suits me. Nothing personal. And I shit on Ilya. He ditched his bank with his own hands. And then, when I saw that bank building... A handsome mansion on the river quay. I love it, well done and lovingly preserved. Those oak doors. Every door handle in brass, and tasseled, with a wonderful river view from the window, and a pier and a church across the river. And the public gardens neighborhood. So quiet over there. I just looked at it, and gasped. And I told Victor, *There, I'm taking this bank. At any cost.*"

I started getting the idea. Victor needed this bank to pull out European funds. That was his interest. Victor himself didn't have a cent, not now, that's for sure. And he had nothing to his name but this old toothless banker. And as such, he wanted a bank he could seize with his bare hands. Just grab it. A bank with debts. A dead bank.

Victor was speaking quietly, without taking the cigarette from his mouth,

"So you, Peter, get your seat in the bank and the signature authority. What's next?"

"And here's what happens next, Victor. I won't bring money in this bank," he replied. "Why should I? I'd better buy gold. I can get it on my own from the Central Bank. The bank sells, I buy. This is a purchase contract and I'm not sharing it with anyone. Why the hell should I share?"

"And why gold then, if the operation is planned through a correspondent account in Europe?" Victor shrugged.

"Listen there, Victor. I wouldn't like to bring the money into the bank unless I'm the chairman of its board. I want to make it so that Ilya could not make a thing of it. Let's say, I got ten million dollars on a correspondent account... "

I felt my cheekbones cramp and my mouth sore with the ghost millions.

"I'm now drafting the bank legal capital," continued Peter, "that is one million, and nine million, for deposit. What kind of indices are these? Can we operate on this much? Both the legal capital and deposit shall be put into transaction... "

"Can you put the bank's legal capital into transaction?" I specified more for my own knowledge.

"That is dead money. So why should it lie idle like that? Money should flow," the banker responded with a toothless laugh.

"Shall we smoke?" offered Victor, clicking his lighter and drawing in on his cigarette.

"There, look," Peter leaned in for a light, and his forehead revealed his strained wrinkles. "I run the first transaction. A purchase of gold. Done."

"Why the hell?" asked Victor.

"Why the hell?" spluttered Peter "Is there any deposit? Sure. The certificate of deposit. Is this an instrument? It is. Is it functional? Oh yes. These funds are kept on a correspondent account. However I cannot take it, as it's metal. Metal it is! And so none of the board members could get it. But this is still money."

"The bank won't issue gold to you," Victor objected.

"And the hell I care!" Peter blurted, "What I want from the bank is only the certificate of deposit."

I thought this was true. Only a certificate of deposit for gold was required. A certificate with the full bank responsibility and liability as to the gold kept in the bank. You only had to negotiate favorable terms and we could start working. And according to him, unless he has the signature authority in that bank, all funds he may draw in the bank would get pocketed by the board members. But this won't happen with gold. And CDs are as good as money, fully operable. Peter cut it fine. Only thing is, he got none of the ten million dollars yet. My gut tells me so.

The banker poured out some more cognac; we drank it and smoked again.

"So how about the feasibility of this, Peter Petrovich?" I asked.

"Quite feasible. The license won't get suspended."

So then, I kept reflecting while smoking again, *Victor tailors this bank for himself. But how?*

Yes, Peter could manage to prevent the bank license suspension. But maybe the board prefers to drive the bank to bankruptcy, grab whatever remains of it and run, rather than give it to someone else. The chairperson would fight to the bitter end for his own interests. No. No good relationship with the Central Bank could help it. Live money was the solution. Rich bundles of crispy green dollars. And Victor had none. And my god, where did he pick up this banker from?

He looked like a scrap yard fellow frayed and toothless as he was.

Peter's reasoning was bold and clear.

"My first step is get my butt properly seated over there. And I wrestle away the chairman. Take over this bank. I tell him in simple words, *Would you like, Ilya, to just sell your gold and go to Monte Carlo?* I know he wants to, no doubt. And that's it."

To Monte Carlo! And I remembered I'd seen that bank chairman once. Ilya Medvedev. He was photographed on my memory. A well-presented old gentleman, tall and purebred like a stallion, in his seventies.

"Yeah, sure, it's high time for the old man to retire to Monte Carlo. Why should he go there? It was not at all so easy... " I wanted to say.

"Well, let him go to the Canary Islands," shrugged Victor, "Or let him just go to Hell!"

I was left wondering why they decided so easily where this old man should go with the case of gold that he'd had to receive in compensation.

The banker, hurt, also came to wind up,

"That son of a bitch Ilya. Keeps getting in the way. Telling me now, *Peter, you come up with the cash! Give me twenty percent for the reserve fund.* I've had enough of him, sick and tired of him. And then, what else would he ask? Not taking care of his bank properly. Not giving a fuck about that bank. What's there on his mind? Not clear. He ditched the bank. So why is he coming in at all? With other things coming into his mind? You do something about him, Victor."

"So what do I do with that senile old man? Go talk to him in the sauna?"

"Why, maybe kill him," Peter said discontentedly.

I was thinking, *It's over an hour I'm here, and still not getting anywhere; how they are going to take that bank?*

"Taking over the bank is not a problem. The problem is money," I remarked cautiously.

"Money is not a problem," Victor cut it off.

You're a bullshitter, a conventional thought flashed through my mind.

"Ann, let me explain it to you. Look. Well, I want the seal today... " Peter turned to me right away.

"And money tomorrow," I could not stand it and lost my temper.

"Take it easy, here, and drink. Money will come," Victor chuckled contentedly, and a shot glass of cognac slipped to me across the table.

"Whatever. If it's sealed now, and money comes in five minutes, this is a problem already," I couldn't believe this outcome.

And no one would. Bullshit, it was. Getting the bank with no cash in hand.

"I've got to take that bank. With or without you," said Victor.

As if just now I fully realized this was mere reality, and that I had already got bogged down there with them. And I had to start working for Victor and Peter. It was no easy matter for him. He was on the edge. The buoyancy of Peter was also somewhat hysterical, his toothless mouth only looked soft. If need be, he would bite into the throat like a bulldog. He found it hard too. He was not so young. As he came to the bank, no one would show him the balance sheet or serve him coffee, was it what he said?

"I'll put it in simple words," beslavered Peter, "the bank is a piece of crap. They only do money laundering, and sack public funds. Embezzling has to be done professionally. Bluntly, steal ten million is to be soft in the head."

"You tell Ilya, *So that I don't see you anymore tomorrow. Or you get handcuffs. Or the public prosecutor comes after you. Or I just commence a criminal proceeding,*" Victor threw off.

"Well, the prosecutor himself won't be coming," Peter's face and mouth softened.

"His deputy then."

"No you listen, Victor," Peter jiggered, "the bank situation is not a simple matter. And we don't know for sure. And then we can do nothing, be that the prosecutor office or other."

"You can do this with money," I got my message across, simple and clear daylight, and looked at Peter hopefully.

"With money?" The old man asked again warily. "We don't know. What if the bank...?"

"And what is there to know? The bank got nothing but debts. And we'll get their debts," Victor tipped his chair backward, clicked his lighter and covering his face with a palm, examined us from under. "All of the bank debts. All the debts should be in a single pair of hands, otherwise we can do nothing."

If I got it right, part of the debt could be taken on a debt management. A huge debt portfolio accumulated by the bank against certain defense companies. And part of this debt, Victor and Peter could started buying. They were buying such debts on some other European banker's money. Victor said this was a friend of his. But who knew? He may have his own interest to pump money into Russia, but wanted it coming through his own bank.

So the major debts remained. And negotiations on these lay with me, as I used to know both managers of the defense companies in person.

Not just happened to know.

Some fifteen years ago, when Arcady wanted the defense contracts, Sergey came and putting the contracts on the table, merely looking at me said, "I'm taking her for the weekend, and will bring her back Monday."

That was it. Later, I asked Arcady why Sergey took me like that without looking. We had not been acquainted. Arcady responded, to know I was well-bred he didn't have to browse me much. This was more like smelling someone of his own kind. In time it all concluded. I wouldn't say that the contract had brought us together with Sergey. I just didn't know what I wanted. I still wouldn't know. All my life was back-ass-wards.

Peter Petrovich reached for a bottle, poured the cognac again and smoked.

"We'll buy this debt now... " Victor took out the papers and offered them for me to see. "This is a draft agreement. These are the terms. You go right now. Suggest that Sergey Sergheevich should sell the debt. Speak to him in person. Otherwise it'll drag on. If he can, let him give his answer immediately. Then you come back. I'll give you the same agreement with all applicable bank details. If he declines, come back anyway. I'll get the agreements ready. You come back by all means, you got me?"

My ass, I reflected indifferently, shutting the door.

CHAPTER FIVE

ILYA

Leaving the gate, I waved my hand, seeing Igor on the boulevard.

"You've been really long."

"Yeah, they turned out to be good chaps, both."

"What did they offer?"

"Here's the agreement. I have to speak to Sergey Sergheevich about buying his debt. I actually feel uncomfortable doing so. I haven't seen Sergey for fifteen years. But you never know, maybe this money is what he needs right now? That's the biggest debt of the bank. And Sergey hardly gets a better offer. Let's go."

"It's all the same to me where I drink my beer," shrugged Igor.

I called Sergey. He said I could come right away.

We passed a couple of stations by metro and then walked along the highway to the design engineering department building that used to belong to an aircraft factory. The glassed-in facade was covered in dust and the building looked deserted, life hardly flickered inside.

"So what? It wasn't the owner of the forged US Federal Reserve Bonds, was it?" asked Igor.

"No, it wasn't him. Victor offered me a job. He intends to capture a minor bank on the verge of license revocation by buying up all the bank debts for a song. He's taken some of the debts into administration and he's got an inside man in the bank, Peter, so he's waiting for him to get the authority to sign, and then... "

"Well, and what people are supposed to do with this kind of bond? That is, in case it were real."

"You mean how to palm it on Mr. Greenspan? Oh, we could try it. Of course he would be rejecting it, asking for its parent documents and the record of you getting it. But still, one could somewhat press on him, make a bargain with a reputable international organization Greenspan should reckon with, such as the London Court or Vatican, and... whatever they got there. No Igor, one cannot pay off this bond, but there is a number of other options," I smiled.

"And what other options are there to make money on this bond?"

"Easy. One could go to a solid bank, surely not the Barclays where you are likely to get a kick in the ass right away, but somewhere more simple, and request the bank would store bonds and issue a safekeeping receipt in respect of these bonds. Clearly, you make arrangement with the banker and share the profit, since your confidence game running up and down the ravines with his safekeeping receipt shall be covered with that bank fair name. The paper the bank may issue in exchange for this counterfeit bond would be a decent document. See, under the law the bank shall bear no responsibility for the authenticity of any documents accepted for custody, but a reputable bank would still wish to trust its customer and naturally accept for custody anything you have, provided you also have some oil contract."

While walking along the deserted corridors of the engineering department, I kept cursing myself for accepting this middleman mission. I felt bad about seeing Sergey. I was scared he got old, or otherwise changed, and would feel bad about seeing me. My face was still looking boyishly bony, same as when he was teaching me to pilot a single-engine aircraft in a small airfield near Moscow. He must be teaching his kids now.

Sergey met me at the door of his office. He hadn't changed; I felt better.

I laid out the draft agreement in front of him and briefed him on the terms. This was a good deal for him. I said the matter was urgent, and Sergey could solve it right away. It would be uncomfortable if the papers stuck with the accounts. He hardly looked at them. Told me to make myself coffee, and went to phone someone.

Relieved, I was thinking thank god Sergey didn't ask me how I was doing. He hardly even looked at me. He must have understood everything without glancing at my worn out shoes.

Sergey went into the corridor to smoke with me. He was still not speaking. That was strange.

We came back to the office, and his secretary called from the reception, *Ilya Ivanovich Medvedev is here for you.*

Oh, that was the point! Sergey was friends with the bank's board chairman Ilya. What a suck. I couldn't just leave. I'd have to play the fool or they start suspecting me.

Ilya came in the doorway in a split second. His jacket was unbuttoned and his white shirt offended the eye in the scantily-lit office. He was tall, lean, and intelligent. He was well-trained. He had the practice to carry himself, to be in the foreground, the social polish and habitude at semi-official events. This habitude had developed over years. And this habitude was striking to the eye. Unwillingly, I pictured him changing into a fresh shirt. He must have lived a long time abroad. And judging from his age, around seventy now, he was close to the intelligence service.

Of course he was an old man now, with a pale face, even whiter than his white shirt, and hunched shoulders. But his posture still preserved the dignity that went with so many who'd been through the times of impoverishment. All these men were similarly grey and swollen, somewhat as beaten in as remote villagers. They, like the trees along the road border were gnarled with the wind.

"How do you do," he nodded to me, accepting a glass of cognac poured by Sergey. "Who's buying up the debt of my bank?"

"I'm not ready to speak about it, sorry."

"The hell I need your sorry! How much you want? A hundred dollars enough?"

"And a stick lolly... "

Ilya, having realized the conversation may take a long time, settled at the desk. He said the debts to the defense companies were the biggest. And I would have bought two of those if Sergey hadn't warned him.

"Part of these debts have been bought already," I couldn't understand why Ilya was asking me who was buying the debt of his bank and why he came there. "Why wouldn't you speak to those who have sold the debt and find out about the buyer? You'll save a hundred dollars."

"Look what you brought here," Ilya grabbed the agreement paper from the desk, crumpling one of the page corners in his fist, "this is a draft agreement with no bank details. You know what bank details will fit here?"

"Nope... "

"Dresdner bank. All clear?"

This wasn't about negotiating. This was a takeover. And he wouldn't know who was buying his bank's debt. The debt would be bought out by various European banks. And what to do in this situation was also clear.

"I don't think it's difficult to pin the bank down by a huge, dud self-debt... this is normally done when someone is buying up the bank debts," I knew I shouldn't say this, he knew it all himself anyway, but the silence stretched on, and I felt stony under Ilya's stare.

"This is what they expect me to do, to initiate criminal proceedings. They expect me to start moving out money from the bank," remarked Ilya irritantly. "Well, you got any other options? Bitchen, I'm ready to sit here till night and listen to you!"

Ilya stopped speaking, still looking straight in my eyes, looking as if he was sick and tired of me already. I was thinking things were turning ugly for his bank, if he decided to come in person.

Ilya picked the phone. He was probably talking to his security guys, as he responded readily,

"No, this is a middleman... A female... "

He raised and said goodbye to Sergey. We left for the corridor. The door slammed.

"Will you sleep over with me or with my security?" Ilya asked me freezingly.

A cold shivering came over me. The deuce knows what kind of security he had. And, if not for Sergey, I would be already getting fucked by his security people. Damn... Stop... He said... Sleep with him? With his grizzled eggs? Oh my god... Thought I misheard that. I took a rapid glance at Ilya and realized this was true. Good heavens, what a shithouse...

"With you," I gasped thankfully for him leaving me the choice.

"Let's go," Ilya took me by the neck and I felt myself a puppy. "My driver will take you to the summerhouse. Make the diner. I'll come there by eight. We'll talk."

Before I could say anything he gave me a sign to hush up, and dialed some number,

"Konstantin, hello. Anna is coming. Please give her a hand in making dinner... Thank you... Anna has recently joined the Bank Board," smiled Ilya. "I had no other choice."

I kept silent. It passed all belief, what he was saying.

"Here's a hundred dollars," Ilya handed me the banknote. "Buy some food."

After a slight pause, he inquired,

"So who is buying up the debts of my bank? Will you tell me now, or after we sleep together? You may call me Ilya," he bent to me smiling, waiting for the response.

His smile left no doubt he'd get the response. His smile was so sharp I could cut myself. I diverted my eyes a bit, and his eyes were right there close to mine. His eyes were dark and wet within low eyelids, dark grey and black at the edges like burnt cigarette ash, calm and dismissive, with swollen lower lids, rimmed with fine lines over the sunken cheeks. He had a high forehead with bald patches of white receding hair. A couple of furrows disappeared within his mouth corners hiding as a smile. He smelled of good cognac. If not for this sharp and freezing smile...

"You never know who you go to bed with, in these bad times, do you, Ilya?"

"Don't be silly. We've already slept together. It's already happened. I never get it wrong about women, if she likes me or not," he said, milder.

I was thinking, *You're such a bastard.*

He reading me like a book. I didn't even have to look at him with hungry eyes.

I said out loud,

"Ilya... here and now I just can't do it... You won't believe what kind of mess I got into... "

"I'm sure of it," he smiled.

"...I wouldn't mind. Why not have dinner and sleep over? My pleasure. Only not here and now... I forgot to buy condoms... "

"Sweetheart, tell me who is buying up the debt and go to Hades. I'm changing the Board for the third time. I want the name."

"Ilya, I've got a lot of my own issues. And you've got your security unit and all you need. You'll sort it out somehow."

"I'll sort you out right now. I've got five minutes yet. So what happened with you?"

We left for the street and came up to his car.

"Someone lost a bearer bond. I wish to give it back. He must be looking for me."

"What value of bond?" asked Ilya.

"It's a million dollars, but it's a forgery. I don't know who is looking for me, but I know they'll find me fast. So excuse me... "

"Forgery?"

"Yes, an art historian told me so."

"So how will they find you?"

"I left my number by the dead body. I have no wish to be in his place."

"Yeah, that is pure shit. So this is why you got that ex-colonel face guy on the bench with you?" Ilya nodded in the direction of Igor, who was sitting in the dim shade cross-legged, peacefully drinking beer and scratching his hairy chest under his open shirt.

"Yes. That is my friend."

Ilya waved his hand to Igor, calling him to come,

"Son, I'm taking her for the weekend to my countryside house. Will bring her back Monday."

Igor peeped into the car, nodded to the driver as if checking up something for himself, and unbendingly told Ilya,

"Take her if you wish."

I thought I misheard something and looked up at Igor to make sure. He pulled my sleeve a bit, *Just a minute,* and quickly whispered in my ear, that Ilya's bodyguard had worked for the Mossad, and if Ilya wanted to kill me, he would have done it already. And Igor walked away down the street.

Ilya turned to me,

"You were never thinking how your last day would be, were you? So think about it. Tomorrow is the weekend; we'll spend a couple of days in the countryside. I'll cook something for lunch tomorrow. We'll go to an old shooting ground and fire at bottles. You'll like it. So what are you thinking?"

I was thinking something different. Such silly thoughts come when you've got to think fast. And I couldn't think fast, so I was in bills trade and not in shares.

Ilya didn't want me. This was clear.

But I was a good option for the men of this kind, older men. I'd be forty soon, but in my twenties I used to have the same kind of men. These men wouldn't lose their time. I was used to this. This was what I actually liked about them. It's not that there were no other men, but I wouldn't remember those others. Men under forty didn't exist for me. I was looking through them as through glass. They were of no interest to me. They kept clinging to those little things they had, their reputation and career, and wouldn't know risk on a grand scale. They were all too greedy, and did not understand how little it actually took. They were all so cowardly, scared to stay in an odd place with ten dollars in their pocket. They didn't know a thing about respect but knew only fear. They were no men of principle, and in case they had any, those would fall out like chicken insides at the smallest pressure. They were just nameless dicks, there were so many... They were all too thrifty. They had a price tag for anything. When seeing my price intentionally displayed on the indifferent face, they would draw in. The older men hardly ever retreated. They wouldn't try to assess my value, wouldn't examine my worn out shoes and wouldn't think of their account with me. They just liked me.

I never dated men, and never received compliments, never had the desire to appeal to men, and never wore high heels. If the man was not speaking of sex within three minutes of our conversation, I lost interest in him. My sex was on the office desk, in the ladies' room, on the windowsill, in the stopped elevator... All brokers were the same. This was common for any company. This was fast easy cash and a quick zipless fuck. There was only one rule – no sleepover with brokers like you, the management only. But I followed the same long before I came to the stock market.

As for Ilya... If I were making my career in a front office, I would bite into him like a pit-bull. Today... no. There was no time to think. And he wasn't asking. There was nothing to think of.

Ilya could as well find out who was buying up his bank debts without my help. In any case, this would be the task for the staff of his bank, this was not his mission. Though, Ilya was the only person left between the bank raiders and the bank. Why wouldn't he leave the bank and retire?

So he wanted the bond paper. That's the only thing he came for.

Oh, damn! So he came in person. I was thinking some young manager would come to produce his papers for that bond. No one had called me till now. He'd decided to handle me on his own. So what was next?

It was interesting what came after sex? The head start was not so bad. It could not be rejected. And why reject it at all?

Smiling I said,

"Yes, I agree."

"What I like in brokers – they know to think fast," harrumphed Ilya. "So see you tonight, baby," he leaned to me and kissed, casually. But his breath smelling of cognac burnt my throat as dryly as a gulp of pure alcohol. "Now we go," he nodded to his driver, banging the car door.

CHAPTER SIX

THE SUMMERHOUSE

Boris, the driver, who from afar, one could guess was a retired officer with a history of service in Western Europe with some embassy, still preserving the polish and following closely.

Boris said by food he'd meant getting cognac for the local neighbors; the rest would be bought by Konstantin.

Konstantin... In the car, putting a bag full of cognac bottles at my feet, I started realizing in the summerhouse I ought to explain to a total stranger, maybe a banker himself, how I'd happened to join the Bank's Board of Directors.

The car was hardly creeping down Rublevka highway, past the stopping busses and trucks, past the brand new tile roofs with the satellite dishes, past the grey concrete fences spit with the fresh roadside dirt, past the new restaurants and other fancy new buildings, beyond which one could see the thick pines blacken.

We came to Nicolina Gora at twilight. There was a regular summerhouse made of old bleached beams. Through the apple-trees the house looked like a hay pile, its roof shining in metal grey. A porch snuggled beside the house, settled under the thick bullis vine shoots. The windows bore white curtains. From a distance, the inside looked covered with snow.

Our feet crunched the sand. There was deafening silence.

"It's so quiet," I smiled at Boris.

"Ilya likes this house for the silence. Even the dogs aren't barking at him... " he said.

The house was roomy, or showy at one time, and today just old-fashioned. Everything was yellow, canary-yellow, and golden, and therefore warm. There was light wood and heavy unpolished furniture. The lamps with old fabric lampshade were dropping their foul golden dust all around. This light appeared in autumn when the sun is low in the milky damp haze.

At first there came a wet and stagnant reek of uninhabitable stale property, but once we lit the fire it vanished into the bittersweet smoke of the birchen firewood, and then came the fine fragrance of wax. I was getting weak-headed with this smell of my childhood; my mother used to fire the stove of our roomy wooden garrison house in the outskirts of Moscow.

With this smoke it felt like late autumn.

Behind my back there the felt-lined entrance door gasped. The birchen wood was plunked onto the pavement next to the fireplace. Konstantin, a squat and chunky man, broad-shouldered, in his sixties, with a round face glowing of health and small eyes, said he lived in the neighborhood, and made himself known as an economist.

He brought us two heavy bags of food. We were making Hungarian Meat, and kept chatting merrily while cutting the sweet pepper, mere chirrup. Thank god he was not asking questions.

As soon as Ilya came, we sat down at the table and had a glass of cognac. Konstantin said,

"I didn't want to ask in your absence, Ilya... " and he turned to me. "So how did you happen to join the Board?"

"The third team came, Konstantin," I started, "but the bank is not so hopeless. I still think we could win the Central Bank and FinMin authorization for ad additional issue of the bank shares... I managed to pull in a million dollars through Nikita Dmitrievich," I added not so confidently, having decided to deal with my headache on my own.

Unwittingly I ran my hand across my chest feeling for the shirt. Its fragile white eggshell was my only overall. It kept protecting me like body armor. This time there was no shirt. My fingers only tousled a T-shirt, which was like I was nude.

Ilya, smiling, gave me a sign to stop, at the proper time. Otherwise I would have told I had a UBS-confirmed billion-dollar deposit, which would border on the insane.

What I'd already said was enough to discourage Konstantin from making further questions.

"Uh... Nikita Dmitrievich, Vice President of Wells Fargo... "

Habitually I thought at the back of my mind, *Good, you know that, you old buzzard...*

We started playing poker, had more cognac, and the conversation took the sideline. But I was still touched on the row, angry with myself, and Ilya, and willing to make a trick of some kind. And, more to the point, I felt that being so angry I could hardly restrain my temper and let something slip quite unwillingly. Especially when Konstantin started telling of Count Leo Razumovsky having won at cards from Prince Alexander Golitsyn his wife, the beautiful Maria. The marriage got dissolved, and Maria got engaged to Count Razumovsky and lived with him happily ever after. What a deadly dull story.

I had a similar tale. It was tingling on my tongue. A friend of mine's grandparents were an old cultured couple, both in their eighties. The grandma wore a lace collar and well-coiffured hair. The granddad wore a waistcoat. In the evening they played a four-handed, pleasant plaintive polonaise on the piano, *You remember infesting me with syphilis, you bitch?* The granddad would scream at the grandma all of a sudden.

I could hardly refrain.

About eleven at night Konstantin said goodbye.

"So who is buying up my bank's debt?" asked Ilya, changing countenance, so that I felt cold with his whiteness.

"Ilya I can't tell you. I'm a middleman and there is another middleman behind me. You find out if you wish."

"I got no time for this sentimentalism, so go fuck yourself... " he smiled as if seeing me through. "And you are still there. You can't leave me like that. Am I right? So," he poured me cognac, "drink this and think what the hell you are doing here. Don't take long. And let's go to bed. I'm tired. So what do you think?"

"I'm really fed up, Ilya! You are not at your front office!"

"Let us not clear up who is going under whom right now. We'll do it in bed... " he paused for a moment. "Oh, wait!" he seized my wrist till it ached. "My front office... I don't fuck in my front office. The front office is fucked in by one and all. The third board is coming to the bank, and every one of them keeps fucking in the front office so one may catch up a clap easily. So I go to the loans office. They turn down everyone... " he smiled to his own thinking. "Everyone knows it. And if someone doesn't know, this must be a newcomer employee. And not just a newcomer. He's either married or isn't up for sex. Most probably isn't up for it. Cause if he were up for it, he would go to the front office anyways. And there he would find out who I'm riding. In the bank, the news spread faster than getting the clap... So who could be the man? Peter Petrovich, my deputy... "

A thought flashed through, what a shit! He was too fast to guess that about Peter Petrovich. If I'm not leaving now Ilya will pull out everything I knew, get me undressed, and then wipe the floor with me.

I gave him a glance. In the deep dead twilight everything white on the table, the cups and the plates, was blaring under the lamplight. Ilya's face got still whiter and froze. There was no trace of astonishment, annoyance or doubt. He was just considering what to do with Peter Petrovich. He was somewhat smiling with his own thoughts. I felt cold with this smile of his. It was offending the eye just like the bright white lighting. I wouldn't want him to turn and look at me with the same smile.

"I'm leaving, Ilya. Thanks for the dinner... " and I ended the phase to myself habitually, *You son of a bitch.*

Taking a step to the door, I looked back at Ilya. He was staring at me as if reading my face.

"You aren't going. You make me sick! Give me the cell," he thrust out his hand.

I looked at Ilya. His face went whiter and sharper. I was thinking, *He will whip away my cell anyway…*

"Your cell, you bitch," he quickly pushed me off the door, wrestling my throat with his elbow, snatched the cell and threw it into the glass of cognac.

For a split second he seemed to think about head butting me. But instead he kicked my shins. Falling, I gripped his arms and he fell down over me. His palm landed under my head.

"I'll strip your bank to the buff," I hissed in a fury right into his cold face.

"I'll strip you," Ilya pressed his elbow to my throat and laughing, started pulling off my jeans.

CHAPTER SEVEN

THE REPLICA

Coming to our senses by noon, we stayed in bed. I was hugging Ilya; my body was aching with sweet lassitude. It was raining hard outdoors, and there was a wall of rain, playing in the daylight like glass.

"You getting up?"

"No. I'll have a nap. Just go wee."

"I'm joining you."

"Coffee?"

"No. I want to sleep."

Falling asleep I was thinking the war was over for me, for just one day. No matter. This day I could be anyone and whatever I liked. And there was no point in being better than I was. There was no one to fool. I was there just as-is, a somewhat worn and faded female with a hungry look in my eyes. I happened to land for one day in the life I was seeking. And I wanted to make it last so much. Breathe it in; absorb the wax fragrance with my whole skin... And simply have a break for a while to get a good sleep, shaking off the dreadful fatigue of the endless war for cash money. And understand I could do without asking for a hundred dollars after a meaningless talk about millions. Running after these millions, catching the trace in the eyes of muddy people who had long forgotten how a hundred dollars looked. Digging my hands into a crop of fax sheets, taking each of them in hope to see there a million written in small indistinct print lines, riding my eyes over the fragile brightness of paper, searching and seeing nothing. There was no hustle to tear off the receiver all day, snack thru the lunchtime beside the phone waiting for the call, and when evening fell, crumple the papers in my hand to sweep it all to the waste basket.

It seemed I had long ago stopped making the difference between reality and that bare air. I kept biting into that wasteland, sinking my teeth into it, and there was actually nothing to crunch my teeth against. If there was only a grit of something worth it all... No, it was mere wasteland. Vast and empty spaces of paperwork were going through my hands. And this empty space was in my mouth, ground over a day so long I could feel its sickly bitter taste.

And for all that, deep down inside I realized I had something nobody else had. I would never stop running after the big money. There was no point in stopping. So how could that all happen to me, as if my life was over and I knew all of it already? As if I was living my last days on earth, and it didn't matter what to eat and where to sleep? I wanted to accomplish something. And I fully realized there was going to be no other chance. This crazy time would pass by as fast as the low tide, taking all the big fish, leaving just tiddlers behind: petty people, petty cash, petty thinking... And the world will lose the sight of castaway millions, numbers dragging their long tails of big zeros. And hurry-scurry will dust over it all.

Will I continue my living in some way or other? Drinking vodka, and then be drunkenly thinking, *What a stupid fool I was, to have missed the time when things were still possible!* It's all so ephemeral, passing by so quickly. It has already passed. Got to move faster to catch up, running after the flying wind.

But now I could take a little breath. Take a breath just because this was the place where I wanted to stay.

I'd barely risen before I went to make coffee. The dining room table was still unattended after yesterday's dinner. I went to get the cups.

Then right into my cup from the ceiling came a few drops of water. And then another one came into the next empty cup, splashing against the glassware with spray over the table. Before I knew it, the water came leaking from the ceiling in a fine stream, right onto the floor. The water drops were soaking between the planks, flowing across the ceiling and getting heavy, breaking into smithereens against the table, making the spoons jump and clink. The wine glasses were clinking too, getting filled with these drips, sprinkling flecks of sunlight around. All the dinnerware was covered with a fine water spray like perspiration. The tablecloth was wet through and heavy, water dripping from its corners. The water stream flew from the table carrying away crumbs of bread. Everything was splashed over. The bread beaten with rainwater got mushy, and the lumps of sugar became transparent, and melted like ice. Then came the smell of wet plasterwork and some fragrance you only get to feel in spring, with a slight tinge of last year's rotten leaves.

I looked at the streams of water overfilling the mug, spilling into the saucer and coiling across the tablecloth, falling onto the floor.

Time after time I remembered my summertime outdoor table under the apple tree bathed in rainwater and those obsolete newspapers beaten with rain that used to be my father's reading, and his glasses sprayed with the rain, and sparrows' skirring among the rain-filled cups and saucers, taking pieces of bread slush.

How long ago was that? As if it weren't me. Still, so often with my eyes closed I was having the same dream over and over again, with the rain pelting against the wooden tabletop, slate-grey with its time outdoors, splashing right and left, and wet newspapers spread over the chairs, cups overfilled with rainwater, delicately clinking with every raindrop, lumps of sugar on the saucer, wet and doughy bread, a platter of overripe pears, golden yellow with a brownish patina, wasps hovering over it, all flooded with the rain.

From a single raindrop falling in my memory cup there came in waves still greater rings. And I remembered the smell. That was the smell of childhood.

The drops expanded, sinking and splashing into the overfilled cups, bringing all around thin wet and golden clash. The old cups gilded on the inside, with their time-stained and somewhat brownish overripe pear coating, fell clinking onto the plates. I would never cease looking at it.

It felt like eternal happiness.

I never thought I could see my father's house so clearly, and myself baby-like happy, behind those porch windows perspired with rain. Along the window ledge between the pots of bloomy red cranesbills there were my toys, trophy brass, tiny bulldogs. For another moment I saw the wet footworn timber flooring, each and every plank of it, and the doors opening into the rooms. I saw my mum's hands, soft and wet, and her turquoise rings. I remembered the smell of boiled linen, and that of the apple charlotte, and the chickens entering the rooms through the open porch door, dusting down and thrusting out their chests, picking something from the carpet. Mum would shout at them and they would scurry, bumping into each other, gabbling and flapping their wings. Through the doors one could see the yard flooded with rainwater, and my father's mudded Chevrolet.

I never thought all this could vanish past retrieval, all this life of mine. I came to my father's house. My father was there no more. There was nothing left of the trophy things. All carpets and paintings were sold. The house was faded and rundown. The empty rooms were homelike, tracked by the chickens.

A spoon clinked and fell off, upsetting the cup. I shivered, forced my eyes off, and called Ilya.

We went up to the attic to see whether things there also got wet.

The attic was dry. The water was running along the planks under the ceiling from the chimney breast, dripping in the middle to make a puddle, and through the planks leaking down under the floor slab. I looked round. There were lots of things hulking up on one another, sunken raffia chairs, piles of books and periodicals. In the corner there perched an impertinent oil, a mix of abstract and modernist style, in a heavy ancient reddish gold frame. I didn't notice anything to get scared of.

I took the painting and came down to the sitting room. Put it against the wall in the corner, glanced at the signature... and froze. Smirnov.

Why? I could not believe my eyes. And yet the signature was well-defined and legible. Smirnov it was. I remembered Michael saying all paintings by Smirnov were held in his museum in Austria. His family had bought up all of his works to the smallest drawing and sold it to the museum. No other museum or private collection had any.

Could this be a replica?

CHAPTER EIGHT

THE MIDDLEMAN

Bullshit... I had to raze Ilya from my mind, and fast. Just forget him. I started pulling my jeans.

"So strange that your father Arkady. You're not like him. In between sex, you are trading in bills. You tear a throat for a dollar. And you hardly ever sleep over with a man you want nothing from. Men out of money simply don't exist for you. You're like a cat, shameless and pitiless. There is no law for you, except a choice of who goes under who and who cats who."

"Is it so obvious?"

"Oh yes."

"Fuck off... I'm leaving."

"You think you have fallen in love? No. This is your pure instinct. Animal instinct. It attracts people of the same kind, just like animals, from kilometers away."

He was right. I knew when I left these doors; I'd be pestered with sharp hunger.

And I also realized what I wanted to buy with all that millions, the life that Ilya had. But the price was too high.

"In case I come back I may settle with your bank bills unit," I was joking away. "But I think you don't want it, Ilya."

"When I saw you I knew I wanted nothing. Save the trouble. How long have I got to fuck you so you say who is buying up my bank debts? I've been dealing with you for two days… "

Oh shit, that was painful. He had just torn me off like his own secretary.

"You tired? So call for your security then."

Ilya suddenly kicked me under my ribs. I could not hold up, flew off and hurt my ass badly, hitting my head against the wall. You motherfucker, that was right into my stomach. I felt sick. Another blow was into the ribcage. It hurt like hell. With a slap in the face, my head felt kind of weak and fuzzy. My face was burning, my nose bleeding. There was no rage. I didn't feel like weeping. I was hurt too bad. Horrible fatigue came over me, along with apathy.

I felt like hating myself as never before, hating myself for all the impotence and misery. I felt exhausted. It was a long time I'd earned anything. I never had anything at all. It was so clear. Every bank broker could see through me. And he was right. I couldn't change it.

I couldn't get back to work. The market had changed. The brokers, companies, buyers, and sellers were all different now. They all had grown small. They kept fucking each other for tenth of a percent interest, ready to set their ass to everyone at half a percent, and would sell their own mother for one percent. I could not do it. The market had kicked me out as garbage.

Those old men I used to work with were getting rare. The reality of petty cash was burning out the people around me, as fire burns woods. Those younger than me considered themselves smart. And each of them was trying to convince me that making their life in pennies was just fine. They were looking at me in squeamish pity, as if I were harebrained. It was all the same to me. This couldn't wound my pride. And mine was really tender. I had pride and ambition. I had lost everything, but these I wouldn't give up. Living a misery, I wouldn't let myself feel like a beggar. If I had, I would have long ago sold myself. When the last penny is spent and more and more cash is needed, the beggar would sell his pride and ambition, the biggest value he has.

The ultimate disgrace was that after dealing in big money and burning so many times when putting their hands on it, these people would soon forget all about it forever.

So was the petty cash eating their brain so badly? That spoke of their dreadful kill power...

Sometimes I felt I'd gone over the edge. I was living in a world turned inside out with its rotten guts up. And sometimes I just wanted to be like everyone else... Relax, have food, dress up, and buy a car... But I couldn't do that. That meant getting buried alive.

I'm losing my days and years, and would get only devastation and misery in exchange. And above all, I'm losing my flair for money, and my fingers' tenacity... behind the air, behind those disproportionate lines of zeros, there's sometimes a reality looming up, just like a ghost of the past life. I could sometimes sense it under my skin, sensing the money with my whole body.

What is more, I could not forget anything like they do. I could deaden my mind with vodka, regrets and consolation. But I could not forget things, and then in ten years burst into sobs over being too weak to stay where I was. And where was I? I'd reached the bottom. So many times I would wake up and think it wasn't happening to me! It was an uncountable number of times.

I was living and breathing in that million-filled air. And I knew I couldn't change anything anymore. It was all the same to me whether I was going to be a miserable beggar, or suddenly get rich. Nothing would change for me. I wouldn't stop. This was my life, and it was this way. In this life I was making money out of thin air. Emptiness had attracted me like a magnet.

Why was I feeling so bad?

I was thinking I could have a rest here with Ilya. No, he was throwing me out, too. This was common market law.

"Why are you keeping silent? Are you insane?"

"Go fuck yourself." I closed my eyes tight, expecting another blow.

"And in more detail? Who was it that to asked you visit Sergey? Peter Petrovich? Where would that old goat get the money from? Who is there behind Peter? How much is he paying you? Or are you getting your share? Do you actually know how to keep your share in a bank?" Ilya said nothing for a while. "Has anyone ever told you how? Or you're just a stubborn fool? Do you want the money?"

"No! I want to live my fucking own life; I like it. Got me?"

"You bitch," Ilya aimed a blow and stopped. "You'll kick the bucket... "

"I'm already there. I'm dead. I'm a middleman. Garbage of the market. You done?" I started rising up.

"Tell me something more baby," Ilya put a napkin to my nose.

"I'm not sure Ilya. There is a European bank play. I think you've got no time."

"I was thinking about it. Stand up there," Ilya helped me to my feet. "Let's go to the bank."

Ilya's cell phone rang.

"What's up there?" he asked, irritated, "Arcady Soloviev? Yes, put me through... Hello Arcady.

The bond paper? Yes, I'm coming. Yes, Anna is with me," and he released me, "We'll drop in to Arcady's place. I'll take the bond."

"And why haven't you told me anything about the bond?"

"Been too busy playing with you."

"And is this bond is yours, Ilya?"

"Why, you had other people after it?"

"None."

"I'll take it on parole," snorted Ilya, holding out the business card I had left with the courier's dead body. "You take my word on this?"

"No."

"That's a good girl."

Boris his bodyguard was waiting at the junction. There was a box of cognac bottles at his feet.

Beside Arcady's house there was a box van with the doors opening into deep, dark, empty entrails. From its doors removal men were bringing a grand piano sideward. It took me time to recognize it. Five people were hustling around it. It was insupportably black in its glassy blackness, just like a coffin. Next came some bagatelles, candlesticks, and figurines in bronze. After a faint glint in the sunlight, they blinked off into the depths of the box van. I stared, and couldn't take my eyes off the piano.

It looked like my father's funeral. There had been a coffin brought out of narrow doors, and then after it, on tiny red cushions, the military men had carefully brought out all of his honors. They'd lined on both sides of the coffin, and fired the final salute. In the confined front garden cortile, it had gone boom, the glass of the old verandah shivering all over.

"You go there and talk to Arcady; I'll wait in the car," Ilya said.

Opening the porch door to Arcady's house I couldn't recognize the place. There was no one on the stairs landing. So where was everyone? Where were all those voices heard below? Where was the noise of rustling steps from the landing and the cheap cigarette smell?

Arcady held the door open for a porter coming with a mirror. For a split second it reflected my grey and sodden features.

He opened the door to the echoing, empty dark with the twilight from the windows, vast and void.

"So where's everyone?" I inquired.

"Apartment two is sold. So there is no one left. The rats have scattered…"

With a deafening noise the sash banged shut. The hollow booming echo went round the deserted rooms. Then came the rain, knocking at the window.

There were less things of my childhood. Empty space showed through those remaining. Dingy wallpaper opened on the walls. A draught I had never noticed before pulled in. The deserted rooms now resounded, echoing, the parquet floor now plinking with footsteps. You could hear the old clock hand go round with a grind.

"You sold out pretty much everything!" I was looking round in astonishment.

"Yeah, all the junkyard."

"So you think that bond is Ilya's?" I asked.

"Definitely. But this is just between us," Arcady said. "Michael dropped in, leaving us a catalogue of Smirnov's works."

Arcady picked it up from the table, and turning over a few hard glossy pages, opened it on a pencil drawing, a portrait of a young man on grey paper. The sketch was made in a strict academic manner, a three-quarter, with blended shading. The flowing lines of the long strokes accentuated a high forehead with visibly receding temple areas of backswept, fair hair. It heightened the cheekbones, nose, and the swollen lower eyelids... The fine line of his lips was sharply highlighted, and softly effaced to the corners of his mouth, as if hiding in a suspicion of a smile. But the lips weren't smiling. And this line was unmistakable. It was Ilya. I turned the drawing to the window light. It discolored to grey, becoming remote and alien. The paper gloss caught the gleam of the window and the sketch vanished as if it were deep underwater.

There was only a signature left in fine italics: *Erich Wolf.*

I came over queer, and felt my mouth bitter.

"Who's that Erich Wolf?" I asked.

"A swindler, my dear. Few people knew of him, actually. I heard he issued the first Federal Reserve bond forgery; he pledged the same with the European banks and cleaned them out in millions. It was not until fairly recently that someone paid up the public debt in these bonds. I don't know who. These bonds have been in circulation quite a long time on the market. Michael got this bond forgery that came from Wolf. But he does not know who Wolf is. I thought I'd better not tell him the world is so small."

For another moment I tried to calm myself. Maybe this was a mere resemblance? You never know, there were so many people who look similar. And what is this sketch? A sleight of handiwork. And in his features, there was something that was not there anymore, like a tinge of death or something. I was thinking I would see Ilya's face now, this cold face infinitely dear in its coldness, and will understand I was wrong, and feel better. But my mind was racing, and I freaked out. It all seemed as if it were happening to someone else, not me. I took another look at the drawing. It was striking in its similarity.

"I called Igor right away and asked him to bring the bond. He said you were taken by Ilya. What could I think? Why was your cell off?" Arcady shut the catalogue.

Could Ilya be a fraudster, really? This was amazing. Ilya was so much similar to Arcady, as if they were classmates.

Arcady was a well respected man despite the fact he has been living in poverty for ages. He was considered an intellectual and a trustworthy person because he had not stolen a single cent over the fall of the Soviet Union, even while he had such an opportunity. It was all about Arcady unwilling to get involved with that war which was far beyond his means at that time. A colleague of his was killed in the communal hallway. And Arcady was scared, the fear inhabited his soul. He was scared to be yet a major whoreson. And the fear has imperceptibly eaten him, the way the rust pierces onto an old car.

There was a lot more of the intellectual elite killed by the illusion of respectability. They have turned rotten since they could not sell themselves. They cost nothing but kept convincing themselves they were not going to sell themselves as they wanted to remain honest people. What a pleasure it was being an honest man wearing rags, toothless, always asking for cigarette butts and thinking how to do till the next pay day and where to borrow cash from, wondering who could offer them a drink? I was thinking, what actually makes these people be honest? It must have been substitution. They want to respect themselves but realize they are only able to respect themselves for money. Should you have a hundred bucks in your pocket you could have the basic human dignity. Should you have no hundred bucks, sorry you are nothing but low life.

Arcady used to tell a major whoreson was more respectable than a simple honest man. Since a simple honest man is a petty whoreson. The poor keep convincing them that those of better luck and fortune have definitely put stepped on somebody's throat and walked over dead bodies, by killing, slaughtering and suchlike, just because they were thinking of doing the same.

Just like all other honest poor people around me that feared the big fortune as they feared for their mean little souls. They were scared to stretch their hands to it, what if they get cut off? And they also feared speaking of money, what if someone asks to borrow some or take them for a rich person? It was so much easier to sit their neck in the poop and never lift their head up!

Deep inside I could hear Arcady's voice, *If I have to make my choice, I'll choose a real whoreson, and not an honest person. Believe me, I am fed up with those honest persons.*

And this was not just words. I have been all this time with Arcady and knew him better than anyone else. Arcady was a noble man as he a whoreson was to the highest degree. And there appeared to be no law he would not cross. One cannot be a true noble man without being a whoreson in spirit. Why so? Maybe because a whoreson would not coerce his nature and lives the easy way as a wolf in the woods. And an honest person would coerce himself into being honest.

I had no wish to know this about Arcady, well no; there was nothing that could repulse me in his case, quite on the opposite. The point was I have taken over that nature of his to the full. And I had no wish to look inwards. I had no wish to see the beast inside. He lived somewhere deep inside there, sleeping, and I had no wish to face him. However, when required I could wake him up with the words, *Daddy!*

And he would tell me what to do.

My men were all like Arcady. And I used to part with them as they could sustain no comparison with him. And Ilya... I could only dream of Ilya, yet a lot better was to get him out of my mind as a mere fantasy.

"Ilya wanted to know who was buying up his bank debts. I'll handle it myself, please... "

"Hurry up there. Ilya is older than me," dropped Arcady.

"Arcady... " I didn't know what to say.

"Let your boyfriend come upstairs. I'll give him back the bond and smash his face in."

"Thank you. You are the best father," I kissed Arcady, and said goodbye.

Making it down and holding the car door handle, I saw Ilya's face through the window. It appeared dim and shadowy. The glass caught the flecks of the rain like glossy paper. And through the glass his face was just like that of the pencil portrait. Detail for detail, the same.

I froze, looking into his eyes, and in a changed voice said,

"Arcady is inviting you upstairs."

Ilya took a box of cognac and started climbing the stairs.

When he came back, I asked why he was taking me to the bank.

"There has to be someone else except the security... "

On the way to the bank, occasionally looking at Ilya I was thinking, what if he was that person, Wolf... then... what a bank to fall across, oh dear! In case he was... Even if he were that Wolf some time back... Then Victor and Peter for him were only children in a sandpit.

And oh, damn it, so he wanted to levy his bank with a debt to his own for a million dollars and this just didn't happen.

CHAPTER NINE

THE SHOT

We came to the bank late in the night. There was only security there. Ilya greeted the security guys, and said I was coming with him, and we walked through the corridors towards his office, set at the far end of the first floor.

The darkness was thick behind the windows. His office was facing a small yard with a wrought iron fence along the highway, with a row of trimmed maple trees. Across the road there was a glassy high rise office building, far above the development along the street, with a parking facility in the yard, a pizzeria just in front.

"Stick around here," Ilya opened the glass door of the conference room.

I sat at the glass table and stared dumbly at the reflection of the pizzeria advertisement panel smeared in a bloodstain against the table surface, the office cabinets' glass doors lit in a whitish neon glow of streetlight. I had a headache.

Ilya's steps padded at the far end of the corridor.

A gunshot pierced the night. The walls shuddered, and the table quaked, as if to spit the reflected red light over my face. I ran out the door. The security staff came running down the corridor where everything was still dark. From the far end door the light came bright elucidating Ilya's white shirt. He sat on the floor leaning against the wall in the corridor shattered with chiliads of broken glass shards.

His head was thrown back, and his sharp Adam's apple pushed out from his neck. His face looked white and somewhat dead.

"Ilya Ivanovich, you take a breathe in gently," said one of the security guys, planting his arm under Ilya's head.

The guards held their breath waiting for him to gasp. Such an explosion makes everything inside break apart. Ilya sighed.

"It's all right," said Ilya, and leaning on his guard's shoulder, he started rising up. "What was that?"

113

"It was a launcher shot from one of the windows across the street; they were waiting for you to switch on the light in the office. The shell touched against the window grate and exploded outdoors. They must have been hitting at an angle. If it came in here... it would fly out the toilet window."

"Bring me a shirt and trousers. In the wardrobe on the left side," Ilya requested one of his security people. "So why are you standing?" Ilya turned to me. "Please help me to change."

We went to the toilet. He started unbuttoning his shirt and showered off the glass. Ilya passed his hand over his hair, shaking off the smashed glass, and came to wash his face.

I felt nauseated. Ilya stooped my head to the sink, opened the tap and getting some water, washed my face quickly. Unbending I looked into the mirror at my disheveled hair and my red eyes and my face whitened in the neon light. I had a feeling of having grown ten years older. The reflection bifurcated. I saw another whitened face behind me, that of Ilya's.

"I stayed there, behind the wall," he said in a low voice, leaning to my ear. "Didn't want to hurt you. It was my friend shooting. It'll take those two weeks to deal with this gunfire, and I've got to go to Geneva, and then make a round of a hundred small banks all over Benelux. The bank has to be pumped up with money. I'll make a deposit of Foreign Currency Bonds, and take a guarantee from each and every bank. All those guarantee papers will subsequently get transferred to Deutsche bank. It will issue its own guarantee and transfer it to UBS, and UBS will issue its own guarantee to transfer the same to my bank. This will make about eighty million dollars. Honestly, I don't really care who wants to raid my bank. No one could overbid this amount."

"A hundred small banks? You won't make it in two weeks."

"I'll make it. Some bankers will come to see me in the hotel."

"And what do you do next?"

"I'll settle up with my creditors. That's it. Now tell them you're a trader, and get the fuck out of here. Bye, baby."

The police and the ambulance sirens wailed outside. The mirrors, our faces, and Ilya's white shirt got flooded with flows of red and blue lights. The corridor was filled with the sound rapid strides crushing the glass chunks.

A guard gave Ilya a pair of trousers and a shirt.

"Let me pull on my trousers," Ilya said to a young nurse that came running up to him.

"I'll help you," she gave him a shoulder and unfolded the trousers.

A police investigator peeped into the toilet,

"May I ask you something? Why didn't you enter the office?"

"Just wanted to wee," replied Ilya.

In the conference room the security guards were talking to the police agents. I went to make them coffee.

"Who are you?" asked one of the agents, and thanked me for the coffee.

"A trader," I pulled my business card out of my jeans hip pocket and gave it to him. "I work on the recommendations. Ilya Ivanovich wanted to sell a few bills to some of my clients. I was waiting for him in the conference room."

"Why didn't you switch on the light?"

"I usually take the bills and go. There was nothing to discuss."

"Can we see this on the cams?" the agent asked.

"You can see this. And the rest you can't. There are no cams by Ilya Ivanovich office, that is a private area, no one ever goes there," responded one of the guards. "There is one cam outside only."

The shooter must have been a pro. And maybe he just wanted to give Ilya a scare. The wrought iron lattice only concealed Ilya's office window halfway. This is where the grenade came through. There are few professionals of such high profile, and those would be military veterans. The investigation was useless. Also, between the perp and the client in such cases there were so many middlemen it was next to impossible to trace the tails.

Ilya was taken to hospital.

A guarantee for seventy million dollars came to the bank two weeks later.

CHAPTER TEN

THE PALM TREE

Over Christmas, it was snowing peacefully. It was warm and quiet in the empty house. All sounds were somewhat toned-down, as if covered with deep snow. In the apartment next door, the hole in the roof allowed for a moderate snow bank. It stayed there, not melting down. All the neighbors had moved out. I was still there. I didn't want to change my phone number, losing my contacts, and I wouldn't find another dwelling as cheap as this. I was also late on my rent. My fax stopped spattering; it just died. The building's power was now cut off, and said to be for the holidays only; as there were no people, who knew what might happen?

I felt angry. Affairs seemed to have taken a better turn, and now there happened to be some silly holidays. I had to light candles.

People were getting ready for New Year's Eve. The Garden Ring was fully illuminated. Fairy lights hung over the radiant highway, flowing down the city at night, dissolving into its lights or effervescing as foam over it again. These lights were mirrored in the windows of the houses opposite mine, where in the evening people switched on Christmas tree garlands. A small Christmas tree market in the courtyard was also illuminated all over. Only my house was dark and deserted, the nude black window holes extinguishing the light reflections as if swallowing them into their empty, dark womb.

The telephone was still working.

"Lenya, greetings! I had talks with the second most senior figure in the Rosoboronexport. Not the top. Second top. He is the decision maker. Keep healthy. Happy New Year! You got a hundred bucks for me?"

"Klim? Keeping fit. I've got some stones. No, you haven't got me, Klim. Alexander Geller is number one in the States in operations with precious stones! That's the leading jewelry network in America! Philip Oppenheimer, distribution network De Beers in London... Could you lend me a couple hundreds?"

"Michailovich, salute! Listen, right now the EU parliament made an allowance for two million Euros. It has to be a private sector entity. This is the investment that requires no security. One third is a concessional loan, another third is an interest-free loan, and one third to be written off... Depending on the project's social impact... Happy New Year! Got a hundred bucks?"

"Fedorovich, hello! What have you got? InterRegionGas? Bills? Six billion? So where did you call? Mental health clinic? Their total annual emission is only five billion! You go to hell!"

"Happy New Year, Max! Yes, I'm just back from Switzerland. So what have you got? Diamond Beach stocks? Fuck. Just give me a hundred dollars."

You're crazy, I said through my teeth, cradling the receiver.

It felt as grim as it was airless, while the draught still came from behind the door.

I just hoped my contacts wouldn't guess I was out of pocket. No, they had a nose for such things. They had a damn good nose. I couldn't let them smell it or they'd all scatter away from me, infected with empty pockets. Bollocks to that, I could do no business with any of them; they were all void and bloated.

Too bad it was wintertime. Too bad my boots were totally worn down. I pulled them on and left the house.

Vagankovo cemetery was white and deserted. The pathways were well cleaned. The tombstones were covered with snow, and sleek with the wind. The forest looked naked, like glass; light shone through, effervescent to the core; only the pine toppers were powdered with snow. Only the brass palm tree by the grave of Sonya the Golden Hand was standing covered only in its broad sharp leaves. It looked great in its weird, outlandish beauty. It was slim, straight, and pushy in its outfit among those bowing bare birch trees. It came from another world, where people don't crawl for money, but hold it with dignity. And the dignity was not what they had in their bare goodie ass, but in the money itself; this money, big as it was, was true and real money, smelling of cash. It was somewhere I could live and take root, without looking back at others...

With my frozen fingers I stuck a fifty-ruble note within the pleats of the graceful figure of a Greek goddess under the palm tree. Being free, it froze up in its stony flight, white on the white snow font.

"Mummy Sonya, help me out!"

These words were scribbled with some gnarled hands low on the pedestal. How many times were these words spoken here? Countless times. Robbers and other criminals would put their cash in the pleats of her robe, for good luck. Asking for help. So the petty cash in the goddess pleats never stopped coming.

I was making my way back from the cemetery in the deep twilight. It was bright all over with lights, and my house in the courtyard was entirely dark. The light bleeding from outdoors was bypassing the building on all sides, like a brook streamlining a heavy stone. Small in size, it looked like an island from afar. It seemed to shake and flow in my direction. Or maybe my head reeled in hunger.

At home I spent another hour by my telephone with a bottle of yogurt, making calls on both my landline and cell phones. When I took a break I heard some heavy, solitary steps on my staircase.

I opened the door and looked through the darkness of the landing. Peter Petrovich was coming up the stairs.

"Peter! How are you? Why didn't you call me?"

"Hello Ann. Why call? I came here for you. You get ready. I found a house in the countryside. We'll stay a month there. And then rent a flat in Moscow."

"And why in the countryside?"

"Cause I'm holing up now. I cannot show my face in any bank anymore. I'm sorry Ilya has bullied you so much. I thought I'd be the only one to expose myself. And I did have all of it, interrogations, courtrooms, house arrest... And fuck them all; there were taxmen, brakti, maroon berets, and whatnot... And all of them wanted money... I didn't think Ilya would put his hand to you, as if he felt something."

"Oh save it, Peter, you've apologized a hundred times already. Let it drop... No one knew it would turn out this way."

"No. I can't let it happen again. Has Ilya guessed we ran the money through your accounts?"

"No, I don't think so."

"Initially I could not understand Ilya at all. What was his way to choose where to wheedle the money off? He may rip off whoever. He ripped off a church once. And then it was the Federal

Security. Then I knew. He's got no strategy. It's just when he wants money, he reaches out his hand to take from whoever he wants, without looking. Son of a bitch."

"...You know that time I was thinking It would take you another bit of time, and you could kill Ilya... " I smiled.

"Well, you kind of killed a chairman. You don't kill where big money lies. And you can explain things well enough, making it clear you can disembowel the man to the last ruble, making him understand you are actually stronger. And in case he wouldn't understand you kill," Peter smiled. "I was telling Ilya it was in vain exposing his butt. He ruined his bank with his own hands. And now I think he just wants to rip it off himself. It was not yet the right time for it... I hope to get Victor settled as a deputy chairman in the next bank. I've only got to make a better choice of bank. It will take some time. My credit line is still waiting to be open."

"Your credit line?" I instantly stopped short, to remember how many times I had heard this phrase.

"Yes. Shall I produce the paperwork?"

"The Lord is with you, Peter, and I trust you. What if the credit line gets delayed?"

"We'll grow potatoes," he shrugged. "Well, you get ready. And throw out your SIM card. You won't need any of it. You'll be working on my contacts only. It's smelling of tea in here... make me some tea, be so kind, it's cold in here."

"Who else will be there with us, Peter?"

"Nope. Just you, me, and Victor. We need no one else. It's better that way."

Peter Petrovich was drinking tea, looking at my fax printouts of bills and contracts that covered the table. And grumbling, *What the hell?* He shook them off to the floor. I was getting dressed, scanning my belongings, to understand I wanted nothing of it.

It was sad to leave this apartment. I'd come to love it. I went to close a small window, and somewhat felt the fragrance of Ilya's eau de cologne in the air. A mere hallucination.

My cell phone startled and squeaked. It was Ilya calling. Frozen, I listened to this cell squeak. Before my eyes the splashes of candlelight floated on the window, smearing into a red stain mixed with the far-off headlamps of the cars stuck in a traffic jam of the Garden Ring.

"Discard... " grumbled Peter.

"No. This is Ilya. Let him think I'm not there," I rushed to the toilet, hardly suppressing the coming nausea.

I vomited. Placing my elbows over the toilet bowl I was thinking I hadn't ever known a man who could become the only man I needed in my life.

Peter opened the door a crack. In his fingers he held my broken SIM card. He threw the wreck into the toilet bowl.

"This is all because of Ilya?"

"No. I don't want a one-night stand. I want to live my own life. Every fucking day of it. Let's go, Peter. We've got to make sail. Ilya could have sent a car for me. Let's go fast."

"You're choosing me?" Peter inclined his head, laughing, looked into my face.

"For sure! Oh god, you can't believe it how happy I'm to see you! You just gave me my life back... I'm exhausted. I can't earn a fuck. The market is dead. I thought I wouldn't stand it any longer. Motherfucker on a motherfucker. Can't make money with anyone... " I was thinking it was actually for the best that Peter had seen me through to my panties and there was no need to explain.

"Oh damn, it's hard to deal in big money on a hungry stomach. You know to make porridge?"

"Oh yes!"

We went down the black stairs to the first floor and entered the open door in one of the deserted flats facing the back yard. There was a huge bank of snow under the windows.

"We've got to jump off, Peter."

"You're crazy! God knows what is there under that snow!"

"This is my house. This is just snow. There... " I gave him a hand to climb on the window sill, and pushed.

I jumped off easily, just like birds fly.

We fell into the snow over mid leg.

"It's so soft I'd rather stay here," uttered Peter falling onto his back.

"Shall we smoke?"

I fell onto my back and lit a cigarette, gave it to Peter, and then lit another one for myself. Lying in the snow we were looking into the high sky, pale with the glow of lights.

"Once we take over a bank," said Peter dreamily, "I'll buy a gold ashtray for the smoking room, just like the one Ilya's got in his bank. And hire long-legged girls for the front office."

We were smiling. Quiet powder snow was falling onto my face. Life was beautiful.

Interview with Anna Schlegel, Author of THE DEAD BANK DIARY

I: Why the series' title is THE DEAD BANK DIARY?

A: The dead banks are the symbol of that time. So many banks expired through the national Default of 1998, and carried on after the same in a zombie way. There were too many of those. Why the Central Bank had not declared them bankrupt and let them siphon off their assets? Why the forward commitment to non-resident banks had been paid through the crisis? That is rather a rhetorical question. The Central Bank was involved with the same. Wealthy people were behind those banks.

The book series action starts back in 1998. The time of Default I keep close to my heart, I 'm still living it through. They say, the time of troubles may come and go, while the people it touched still can't stop living it through. Why so? That maybe because life in Russia deserves the case name of Russian ennui that so many classics dwell on. At the time of Default it was done with, and there came the era of overindulgence and outlawry, that is to say, the times of freedom which had never more happened ever since. I am missing those days.

I: Tell me a little about your first thriller THE DEAD BANK DIARY.

A: This is the first novel from the series. You can read each novel independently. There are the same characters. My novels are not based on a true story – that would be stupid – but you will feel the reality. The story is told from the first person; it's me. No violent crimes, or anything of the kind. No politics or 'dangerous' Russian reality. Only MONEY. Beautiful financial schemes and frauds are in each novel. I love the beautiful gray area schemes on the verge of a crime. There will be a hostile takeover of a bank or forced bankruptcy. Raider attacks on banks attract me the most.

I: What attracts you to a bank raid?

A: I saw a bank takeover with my own eyes from the beginning to the end. This had an unsuccessful ending. But there was a moment when Victor said, *Imagine this is your own bank.*

Maybe Willie Sutton felt the same. It was no more pleasant than being in the bank at night alone.

I: Is there really a lot in your writing that has happened to you?

A: Yes, everyone in the stock market knew about it. Before default the banks fell down as a house of cards. Banks were pumped up with money and went bankrupt very easily. It was the period of wild capitalism, and I was lucky that time has passed through me.

I: You write you have been sick with millions...

A: Of course, big and easy money is like a drug. I hid this disease a long time, as alcoholics or addicts do. And then I used as well. Maybe I was lucky that I remained without work. I also realized that I would never get a job. What was important earlier to me lost its sense. I had a hungry look.

At that time I was mixed up. People had lost their former life. It was easy to get acquainted with everyone: a minister, a diplomat, a vice-president of the bank... I felt that time was not so long. That crazy time would leave as fast as a river. It would take the big fish away. It would go down to the depths. Already

131

that time has gone. That time you could catch a big fish with your bare hands. I have nothing to regret.

I: Are these frauds real?

A: Yes, they are true. But to accomplish this you need an insider in the bank. Better someone on the bank board. Or you must get a lot of money to fall down the bank.

I: Is money the main thing in your novels?

A: Yes: if you're wondering how to get money out from thin air, the smell of money, how to reverse off-balance money, how to break banks, then my novels are for you. I write all about the money. The reader will always know what to expect.

I: The main hero of the series is Victor; meanwhile the hero of the first novel is Ilya. Why so?

A: Books are written in memory of Victor, a retired Foreign Intelligence Service officer and a fraudster. I was lucky to meet him. He died more than ten years ago. At the heart of all the novels will be my memories of him.

The hero of the first thriller and the following novels is Ilya, the bank's chairman. He is in his seventies. I imagine that some readers will be turned off by his age. But heroes come from anywhere. Writers sometimes say that characters find themselves. Ilya is a real person. He had become a hero unexpectedly for me. But I cannot tell who this character really is. In any case, all the heroes I've written about are real people. Default time in 1998 has made its own characters. They have been called the children of default. In real life they look like characters in a novel. It seems to me that the real life is much more interesting than any fiction.

I: Your novels are realistic, aren't they?

A: Exactly. While I worked as a market middleman, I made some digital recordings. That's a lot of hours of negotiations. I did not make these recordings for my safety. There is no danger if you know the rules of Russian deals. Did I feel that very sharply at the time? I realized that the time of default would pass away. And to build a business from scratch would be impossible. I felt everything would come to an end very quickly. There were crazy days. I do not know why I've made these recordings. It was done by intuition. My novels have begun from these records. Some conversations were so interesting that they were included in the text with a few changes.

But the novels are not realistic. They are not like 'Liar's Poker' by Michael Lewis, for example. My thrillers are completely in line with the laws of the novelistic genre. Here there is intrigue, the heroes find out something unexpected about themselves, and there is a twist in the end. That is why in the first thriller I have got a US Federal Reserve Bond, face value one million dollars, issued in 1934. A very beautiful fake.

I: Was this bond real?

A: Oh, yes. Some fakes arrived on the market from various backgrounds. One of the most plausible stories says that a box with these bonds was taken out from Germany at the end of World War II. Boxes are gone around the world. So the Fed decided to devalue them. Dresdner bank issued a letter about its ability to accept the bonds. There was one thing: each bond had to have the Treasury Certificate, Global Immunity and Gold Bullion Certificate. But there were not. It's just a beautiful story. They say also that one of boxes taken out from Germany had been opened by one of our drunk generals. But it is known that some the European banks accepted these bonds as a deposit. I haven't held this bond in my hands. I had only a high-quality digital copy. It's a terrific document. And I have seen the parent papers. The stories about these bonds are so various... I told a one in my novel.

In fact, the story of a document from Dresdner Bank seems true. Once a casual acquaintance from special service said that not so many years ago, he unloaded trucks with trophies from German museums, which were brought from Moscow to Tomsk. There were leather-bound folios with engravings. They have not been packed and were unloaded without inventory. They were frozen in the thirty-degree frost.

I: Do you have any acquaintances from special service?

A: Just a few. These are the people from whom I try to be as distant as possible. But time goes on, things change. If someone said that I was seeking an 80-year-old professor, former officer of the NKVD (the People's Commissariat of Internal Affairs, the forerunner of the KGB), and we would have absolutely similar views on life, I would never believe it.

I: Is he Ilya?

A: Partly. Outwardly of course. He was a handsome, 6'5 feet tall, accustomed to getting any woman he wants.

I: And so your hero is in his seventies...

A: Yes, Ilya would not be the chairman of the bank if he was younger. It would be not plausible. But he is a strong hero. He loves risk. Do not worry, the main hero never will die and will not be ill at all. And what the hell can I do if this hero appeared, living his own life? He is stronger than me.

I: Your novels are written from the first person. You are the storyteller and the hero. How much truth is in your words?

A: Not a lot. But I am the reliable storyteller. You can trust me. There are two main heroes: Ilya and me. There is a main hero in two characters. I am the hero who could not pull off the plot. I am the type of hero who is called 'a magnet for shit'.

And Ilya, on the other hand, is the bastard. He breaks all the rules. He cannot be understood. He is not cruel himself. He has his logic. To be with Ilya is like making a deal with a devil. He doesn't need a victory or money. For him there is neither good nor evil. He simply stretches a hand and undresses who he needs. He can undress FSB (former KGB) or the church. He does not care.

Ilya is an outstanding character. I am glad that this hero has found me, and let me to write first four novels, and I hope there will be new one. He is inexhaustible. It's not just a thriller but a love story.

I: Tell me about yourself as a hero.

A: I'm a free trader, without any work, without a family and without any attachments. I've got a father. We met each other when I was a child, and I am happy with him. My heroes have also no family. They have a past, but I do not describe it. They simply live day by day. Each novel is one month in the lives of the characters. A story begins wherever it catches them. There are no memories.

I go on my way following the big money. It attracts me. I am infected with crazy millions. The people like me are few. Time has changed. It seems my kind doesn't exist anymore. I have an outgoing nature. But I love going after millions. It seems I will die on the run. I think I'm going mad. Where will I be on my way? Let me.

I: Are all of you heroes swindlers?

A: Yes, they are ordinary people. There are no good guys. There are no murderers. Losers just stay without money. Money is the most humane weapon.

I: Why are they so?

A: I have the answer in my second novel FOR THOSE IN THE SHADE. They are that way by nature. They just eat each other. Sometimes literally. And there is nothing to do about it. It is simply a life. There is a beautiful and convincing psychological theory about it. It's founder is a Russian prof. Porshnev.

I: You have a philosophical degree. Are there other philosophical theories?

A: Nietzsche and Russian philosopher Berdyaev are closer to me. But in my novels there are no long conversations. My heroes do not sit down with a cup of coffee. Each novel has a theme and a counter-theme. For example, the person is against the tyranny of absolute power, or against the law of necessity.

I: How about you? Are you a badass hero?

A: Of course. But I found it hard to write about myself as a badass. It was real hell. Good guys seem boring and unrealistic to me.

I: How much do you write about Moscow?

A: Not a lot. It's so funny to see how Hollywood films present Moscow as a dangerous city. Moscow does not differ from a European megalopolis.

But of course it is Moscow. I write about that time when the city was flooded with fantastic money. All was on sale: oil, gas, diamonds, public debts... The city breathed big money. I often write about it.

That time has gone, and the city was paralyzed without money. During that time empty buses were passing through downtown. And again Moscow began to choke with million-strong oil contracts, federal programs and cheap bank guarantees. Also there were offers of high yield private placement programs with sonorous names of the Top 100 European banks. With mad percentages. They had nostalgia for those days that had recently fallen. They smelled of the quiet life.

I: Don't you think Moscow is a dangerous city?

A: I understand your question. Well, as dangerous as an arms dealer? Maybe now there is some interest in Moscow, but I would not like to write more about Moscow as a landscape. Of course, my main hero has a bodyguard.

Is Russia dangerous? No. People with ideology are dangerous. Rich Russians have not got it. Ideology is for the poor. The poor cannot make a rich state.

I: Have you had a hard life? Are you writing much about yourself?
A: Not much. But I try to explain what a person feels after he has been gobbled up by a city such as Moscow.

You may also be interested in novels by Anna Schlegel

THE DEAD BANK DIARY SERIES

FOR THOSE IN THE SHADE

Book Two of The Dead Bank Diary Series

ISBN: 9780986174964
ASIN: B014Q92DE6

THE PRINTS ON THE SNOWS OF YESTERYEAR

Book Three of The Dead Bank Diary Series

ISBN: 9780986174988
ASIN: B017KYY2MA

SOME DAY I`LL HIT A BANK

Book Four of The Dead Bank Diary Series

ISBN: 9780998185323

THE FROZEN DEBT

Book Five of The Dead Bank Diary Series

ISBN: 9780998185309

MY GOD IS MONEY

Book Six of The Dead Bank Diary Series

Coming Soon

FOR THOSE IN THE SHADE

Book Two of The Dead Bank Diary Series

by Anna Schlegel

ISBN: 9780986174964
ASIN: B014Q92DE6

---

*You may live your whole life without getting to know
who you are, and sometimes this is for the better*

It was a bank robbery, however this time the gunmen came not for the cash but for the bank itself, and all that followed happened faster than a domino knockdown.

The bank was bankrupted professionally.

Bad debts of the Third World countries, Cuba, Zimbabwe, Morocco, and The Congo have been returned on the bank's balance sheet. Once, the bank sold the debts to itself, to an offshore company.

Who did this?

The banker finds out the bank in Amsterdam... and has taken it over completely.

THE PRINTS ON THE SNOWS OF YESTERYEAR

Book Three **of** The Dead Bank Diary Series

by Anna Schlegel

ISBN: 9780986174988
ASIN: B017KYY2MA

The best to rob the bank is the banker himself

The Bank, facing bankruptcy, fell out of the hands like a snowball rolling downhill to flatten everything under its weight.

Behind every bankruptcy there are people who make it happen. But there are no influential people. Big figures are absent. It seems you stay face to face with the emptiness.

This happens when the Central Bank is playing against you.

SOME DAY I`LL HIT A BANK

Book Four of The Dead Bank Diary Series

by Anna Schlegel

ISBN: 9780998185323

The bomb lives to its internal time

My life became lonely and monotonous, almost mechanical in nature, with a mechanism akin to a ticking bomb. It could be ticking for days and weeks, quiet and imperceptible, to blow up everything around at the right time.

This way common folks used to live in the past, bakers and shoemakers. They lived their lives until the revolution burst out. It was their time. And then they went out the door of their bakery and shoe shop for good to take the ministry chairs and cut the heads off the aristocracy, by weaving plots and intrigues. I knew I will not miss my time.

It seemed to me I could go on for another ten years, and one day stumble on a terse line in the newspaper and realize: my time has come.

THE FROZEN DEBT

Book Five of The Dead Bank Diary Series

by Anna Schlegel

ISBN: 9780998185309

When totally nude have a look, maybe you still got the shoulder loops

One morning he stayed bare-ass, there was no money, no name, no wife, and nothing left... just his shoulder loops.

MY GOD IS MONEY

Book Six of The Dead Bank Diary Series

by Anna Schlegel

Coming Soon

A bank is like a condom, you can only use one at a time

The rats are perennial, they'll exist till the end of times, wealthy and miserable, in the wild or in prison, through any shift in power or regime change, be that capitalism or communism, and nothing would ever alter them as they could adapt for any environment and their world of invisible omnipresence is well protected by their God, and no one would get out of His hand since their God is money.

SPY & FINANCIAL THRILLER

THE SLEEPER SERIES

MONEY CAN`T LIE

Book One of The Sleeper Series

ISBN: 9780998185330

ON MYSELF FOR LITTLE MONEY

Book Two of The Sleeper Series

Coming Soon

AUTHOR'S NOTE

There are no agents and no offices furnished with the electronics, it is free of everlasting arguments with the management and those talks of the crummy salaries.

He's an agent with no support, and he's got nothing on his hands... But then why, if he is a respectable banker in a European bank?

ABOUT THE SLEEPER SERIES

These are the books about someone I met in Berlin, and four days later I had to become his wife and his backer-up, the second key to the deal, the duplicate. It would not have happened if he had not turned into a transient target for the secret services, a mere bargaining chip. He was sold out as a long sleeping Russian agent.

The deal to which Vlad was a shadow partner was tied up.

This deal was about the discharge of foreign debts of several countries in Africa via a number of embassies and ministries, oil companies and stock trading businesses, through the German and Swiss banks... It involved over a hundred different partners, functionaries and security officials, company leads and multiple agents. And they were all hidden behind a bunch of middlemen. This deal was made of personal contacts and handshakes, of non-committal talks and of pure air. Once materialized, the deal incorporated proper ironware and Swiss-clock precision.

Who would not wish to hold this kind of deal in their hands? They were so many. It could make a perfect channel for arms or diamond trafficking.

However the people were the main asset of that deal. So it took us a while to realize in the wrong hands it could play on one occasion only, and that would be to knock out just a single man.

If only we had known this, it would be clear there was no coincidence, there was no token money in that big a game, and every player was worth a lot. Seven digits were invested into this deal takeover, and should they fall onto us in a banking package it would have crushed us like a block of concrete.

That time we were not aware of this. Vlad and I were making time pass in an empty house in the suburbs of Berlin along with vodka and cakes, trying to figure out why the hell the British intelligence had started to look out for Vlad as a Jewish mom?

They say, nothing bands people better than fear, neither love nor hatred.

These novels are not based on actual events but you can still scent the reality in every word.

MONEY CAN`T LIE

Book One of The Sleeper Series

by Anna Schlegel

ISBN: 9780998185330

---

*Should there be three pieces of crap this is of the
British intelligence classic*

One day there happened what may happen to a sleeping agent, he was burnt by the same intelligence he worked for. He expected to be arrested and suddenly realized all those things he felt overwhelming for the last week were nothing but seeming true. And in reality it was all quite different, and he had to save not his neck but the operation to which he was a shadow partner.

This deal left no legible trace. It was just like a woman always staying with somebody else in her pursuit of money. It was made of thin air, of powerful links, of noncommittal talks and handshakes. In this deal every cent was lying in someone's hands. So not knowing the hand that handed this cent over to some other hands one could learn nothing at all, and the whole thing turned to be a number of bulging bubbles of virtual money that disappeared from bank accounts with a single keystroke. It became the reality pulling in to death.

So many people wanted to hold that deal in their hands.

Therefore he understood nothing would happen to him there, he could just walk out with no glance back since he knew so well all those counterparties involved in this operation, and these people could sense something went wrong from miles away and could read it by his walk, there was no need to warn them, they would scatter away on their own and hideaway like rats. And the deal would vanish alongside with them, flowing like sand between his fingers.

If someone wanted to hold down that deal nothing wrong could happen to him. He just had to walk into the street. But then, what if he was mistaken?

ON MYSELF FOR LITTLE MONEY

Book Two of The Sleeper Series

by Anna Schlegel

Coming Soon

The British intelligence cannot compromise its integrity, it will adhere to its principles like in the old times of rock `n `roll. And it's damn good to look at it working... but then it's scary to see it work against yourself.

He was not worth a straw to the intelligence, a mere sleeper, a small coin. One day he felt behind his back there was someone else, someone a big shot of so high value they could not afford to lose him. Who could that be, a recent turncoat? He had no idea.

He could only see a trace of him barely-there, just a tip. And they were seeking to ward the trail off, not just by drawing it aside as now it appeared leading straight to him. So that everything would point to him. The trace would be lifeless, of beautiful classics and as much stone-dead.

ABOUT THE AUTHOR

I was born in Moscow. I studied at the Moscow State University at the Philosophical faculty. I got a PhD in philosophy and stayed without work and without money. The financial crisis began. Some years I was looking for a work, but took it easy. I was a securities trader in an investment company by chance. And then there was the default in 1998. I was without work again.

This was my best time. I became the financial middleman of off-market private transactions. I had nothing. I have been looking for too-big deals. But then there was a time that it was quite possible for me to be the middleman in the sale of a Libyan oil tanker or the sale of aircrafts abroad. I got sick of conducting multi-million dollar transactions and lost all sense of reality.

I met Victor. He was a retired Foreign Intelligence Service officer. He was a magnificent fraudster. I understand how strange it sounds. But at that time before the Yeltsin decree in February 1996 the Intelligence Service was pumped up by money. And

Intelligence Service officers one by one began to hold the post of deputy chairmen of the bank. It had happened overnight. Certainly, I could say: he was a magnificent financier, but... to call him as a financial fraudster would be more truthful.

Capturing the bank was in my sights. The insider of the bank was the vice-president of the bank. I write about his capture almost unchanged. Victor would be recognized by his conversations. Before leaving, he left me his three passports... So I do not know his real name. There were no closed doors for him. He had friends from the federal agency for government communication and information and from the board of directors of Deutsche Bank. All kinds of people.

Years passed. Victor is long gone. And there are fewer middlemen.

I feel myself to be on the way out. The whole generation is on the way out as well, those who are described as robbing the country.

I like those who robbed the country, and I'm pleased how it was done. They were really talented financiers, nothing worse than financiers on Wall Street. They left the country and have taken the money with them.

Since then, Moscow's air did not smell of millions any longer. But it seemed to me, it was still in the depths of my house between a pile of white shirts.

Now there are no more financial middlemen. The young have got jobs first. They receive a salary at the end of the month, and seem to have already forgotten the smell of crazy millions. It's like being drunk. There's a dizziness from it... They did not want to breathe this air. They did not want to poison their lives. They earned their money. They had wives, children, dogs, cars, which it is necessary to care of... Their heads have been overflowing with thoughts of petty cash.

Then the middlemen were old. And I stayed with them. Therefore, the heroes of my novels are in their sixties.

For the former friends who stayed in the stock market I became infected. No, I just died. And I have been smelling of sweet cadaveric decay.

It seemed to me that I was among the dead. And it felt really bad for me as a living being. But I shared their way of thinking. I was the same as they were. Ridiculous and old-fashioned, useless clutter, rubbish. Market garbage.

My friends were precisely the same as a middle-aged gentleman.

Sometimes I catch a strange look at myself, but then forgot about it. The metropolis cleaned me from their memory. There was no need to be as nice as kind people who talk with clients and colleagues daily. I had a different way of talking. My talking always led to a deal. And in case it didn't, I would give the finger and immediately forget the useless person as if shaking off dust. And that's all.

I have nothing to regret. I had nothing to blame myself for. Dogs wouldn't blame themselves for their dog's life, would they?

I could not return back to the stock market. It has changed. Brokers, buyers, and sellers have been changed. They all had grown up a little. They have got each other for 0.1 percent interest, ready to set their ass to everyone at 0.5 percent, and would sell their own mother at one percent. I could not do that. The market has kicked me out as garbage.

And the old, among whom I used to be, are gone. The reality of small money has burnt out people around me as fire burns wood. Sometimes it seems to me that I have gone mad, that I live in the world turned inside out. Sometimes I would like to be like anyone... to have a rest, eat, dress, buy a car...

But I can't do it. It would be a living death.

It seems to me I would lose days and years and end up in devastation and poverty. And I would lose the scent of money, and the skill ... I clung to the sale of oil, diamonds, and bank guarantees, though I'm sure that it was simply thin air and there was nothing behind it. Sometimes I woke up and thought that all was not with me. But I lived and breathed the air of millions. It was my life. In my life I gained money from thin air. Emptiness is a magnet for me.

Now I have got nothing. I do not care. I like my life. I like to go for millions. It's impossible to stop me. I might be put down like a mad dog.

And I still have a sense of money. I can smell the street's air and say that the market has changed. It smells as sharp as the smell of fresh bread from a bakery in the frost.

FINANCIAL THRILLER

THE DEAD BANK DIARY

SERIES

FOR THOSE IN THE SHADE

By Anna Schlegel

BOOK TWO

You may live your whole life without getting to know who you are, and sometimes this is for the better

CHAPTER ONE

MARC

Moscow, July 1999

The night was warm and clear. Ilya was to come the next day and I could not sleep in his absence. I stirred up the burnt charcoal in the fireplace and went to close the door.

Through the dim glass of the door opening from the living room to the terrace, through the reflection of my own sharp and unadorned face, I could see a stranger. The man was standing on the porch. He was a heavy-ass about sixty, big and fat as a wild boar.

"Hello, I'm your neighbor. Marc," he named himself, breathing out his words with the smell of booze.

He looked like a German or of Baltic descent, but had no accent. There was something fishy in his smile, opening a row of small and sharp teeth, with watery, arrogant eyes. I felt confused looking his huge body, bloated face, and inverted, wet lips. I felt ill at ease. Yet this Marc looked quite commonplace, almost as an elderly insurance agent. He seemed invisible, observant, even sleek and loutish at the same time. Such people do exist, – they're grey and unseen, expressionless, – as if nothing has ripened inside, no feelings, no love, no hatred, no greed, no strength... They've got neither good nor evil. But in this one felt long – back over – ripe, as if he had overeaten and thrown up, and was ready to eat more. He was filled up and overflowing. One could see it in his drunken, sweaty countenance, in the grey hair stuck to his forehead, in his manner to stand astride as though he owned the place.

I thought unwillingly, *Oh you're a slut, my dear.*

"Nice to meet you. Anna," I greeted him, opening the door, recollecting having glimpsed him some time before.

"You smell of this house," Marc grinned, as if ascertained all he had to know about me, and changing his tone started speaking in a different, more sober voice. "Someone entered the bank.

Let's go. I'll drive. Ilya has just called. He's already started."

Marc cast the travel bag onto the backseat and took to the wheel. We raced off in the car and in a couple of minutes we crossed into Rublyovo Highway, – glaring car lights slowly coming from the opposite direction. He beeped a horn and went to overtake, showering the rear cars with grit spray from under his wheels from the verge.

"Someone entered the bank? And what about security?"

"The security guy handles the drinkers and dopers coming round after a dose to the bank through the main entrance. This was no common robber. He knew how to hook into the camera surveillance and pass over the alarm system. The alarm was on while he was inside. There must've been two of them. Or more than two. What can a security guy do alone? Light me a cigarette."

"So why Ilya wouldn't call some private security?" I inquired, making nothing of it all.

"So he called me."

"Argh... " lighting a cigarette for him I started viewing Marc's face, spongy as slush bread and unconcerned, still getting nothing.

"In the case that the alarm had deployed, the security would have come. But this time, the professionals came to the bank. The security would only scare them away. We'd better know who we are dealing with, and what their goal is. Why would they come to Ilya's bank? What do they want? The bank's got no major accounts. And private depositors are very few," Marc was speaking to himself waiting for no response.

The bank was small. They call this type a small, single 'pocket bank'. Such banks normally have a couple of good clients who dispose of the bank as if it were pocket change, without scruples. It was clear this time it was no pure robbery case. This could not happen. This was not the bank one would try to rob.

"I can tell you for sure the bank is void and empty," I started smoking after Marc. "Ilya wouldn't keep his money in his own bank."

"So how is he making money then?" chuckled Marc, embedding his car between two other rows in a soft, insistent way like a knife into the butter.

"No way. He doesn't give a fuck about his bank. Ilya would only start thinking of his bank when someone starts pulling the bank from under his ass, you know."

"Eh... I see you know Ilya really well."

"So how did that guy break into the bank?" I asked, lighting another cigarette for him.

"Through the first floor window. He made it down from the roof at the point of Ilya's office. That means he knew there were no cameras... There is one outdoor camera only. Then the security guy noticed that someone hooked onto the cameras," Marc drew in on his cigarette, he was calm but his neck turned red over his T-shirt collar. "You know to shoot?"

"Yes. Ilya taught me, over here on the deserted abandoned firing ground."

"Could you shoot at a human?"

"Yes."

"You don't like humans much, do you?" Marc gave a hum.

"I like cats. They don't come asking you for money all the time," I joked away as usual. "So what? There's someone walking around the bank... And do we know exactly where he is?"

"The security guy remained at his post. The security post is clearly visible through the entrance door. If he walks away he may scare them off."

"Then, the man is walking around the bank... "

"There is another alarm system in the vault. In the case he doesn't know to switch it off, we'll clearly know where he's walking... Might any of the bank clients keep something in a deposit box? Or in the safe? What could it be? Or this could be a hacker... Shit. Light me a cigarette."

When we approached the bank, the road took the bridge. From a distance through the trimmed maple tree crowns along the highway I could see the parking in front of the bank, and Ilya's car. He'd parked a block from the bank quarters in a dark back-alley.

"We'll go to the bank on the same road," Marc said, shutting off the engine next to a residential building.

Marc and me, together we walked along the embankment past the small restaurant of the old wooden river station. It was gently squawking against the water's ebb, slopping with its rotting barrels. It felt cold at the riverside. The old mansion of the bank behind the wrought iron fence was shimmering white between the maple trees. Their globe-shaped crowns were receding, and their carved leaves had a burnt patina. The wind was tearing them and throwing them under foot, crispy and fragile as glass.

On both sides of the bank there were high-rise office buildings. Behind the bank there was a back yard, fenced with a mesh of frost grape from the old high Stalin-era buildings. Through the fine, knotty vines we could see their flaking walls and zinc-coated waterspouts, shimmering in the dark like organ-pipes at church. On the narrow balconies drying linen hung white. There came the smell of fried potatoes and apples.

Keeping to the deep shadow next to the steel mesh, we approached the fire-escape and climbed to the roof. Next to Ilya's office we could see the first floor window had been cut out. Marc took his mountaineering equipment out of the bag. Descending from the wall, Marc nicked into the window and held out his arm for me. We got into a small room behind Ilya's office. Ilya sometimes stayed there overnight and did not want any cameras in that room, or his office. A door from that room opened to the main filing room, where one could get lost among the shelving units. It was quiet in the corridor. I strained my ears to hear the door rustle, or footsteps in the distance. There was nothing. I felt a breath behind my back. It was the wind stirring the curtain through the broken window, and outside, the chilly darkness of the night time street. I felt the nocturnal rawness.

"Where could he be?" Marc whispered giving me his Beretta that I accepted with my hands chilled all of a sudden. "We've got to know fast who we are dealing with. Let's go to the server room. My gut's telling me."

We went into the corridor and walked to the analyst's office. Entering the roomy office I could not recognize it. It was dark and empty inside like a wood before the rain. Or could that be due to the silence where I was scared to smell a breath?

Finally we saw him though a number of open doors. Through a narrow corridor, the analyst's office was connected to the server room, from which another door opened to the filing room. And that one was ajar. He would have exited through the filing room to Ilya's back-office and left the way he entered, by the roof.

He was a masked gunman, squab and slim, middle-aged judging from his stoop and stony, spread back. The mask was hiding his high cheek-bones. He must have been retired Special Force. Across his chest, the man was holding a stub gun. He was standing with his back to us. He must had finished his work, and made for the filing room. Marc gave me a sign to stay behind the door, but I could still see him.

"Stand where you are. Stick'em up," Marc said in a low voice, aiming his gun to his back.

Anna Schlegel has a degree in philosophy. She was Securities trader before the recession. The last ten years she has been involved in off-market private transactions as a middleman in Moscow.

She writes in genre of financial thriller. THE DEAD BANK DIARY is her first novel.

Anna lives in Novi Sad, Serbia.

CONTACTS INFORMATION

_____

For information about the author, please visit TheDeadBankDiary.com, thedeadbankdiary@gmail.com

For information about the published books, please contact Schlegel Press Association at schlegelpressassociation@gmail.com